ENEMY AT WORK

"Stonewall has to be stopped. Your people have one more chance, in Cairo. See that it succeeds. Even then, I'll have no choice tomorrow but to report to Colonel Qaddafi everything that has happened."

Al Hawaadi paled. Even though he worked for the powerful *shurtah*, the secret police of the Directorate General of Public Investigations, mention of the Libyan strongman's name and the reminder of how costly this American stood to the ruler, brought a cold, sick feeling to his stomach. He licked thin, harshly cruel lips and brushed his long, spatulate fingers over the pencil line of black mustache that ran above his lip.

"I will see to it, Comrade Colonel."

"You do that. By this time tomorrow, I want to hear that Stonewall is dead, dead, dead."

#5

LIBYAN WARLORD

SOLDIER FOR HIRE

By Mark K. Roberts

ZEBRA BOOKS
KENSINGTON PUBLISHING CORP.

ZEBRA BOOKS

are published by

KENSINGTON PUBLISHING CORP.
475 Park Avenue South
New York, N.Y. 10016

This one is for *Sir* Sidney McQueen, father of the Sidewinder SMG, genius inventor and good friend. Best as always.

MKR

Lyrics for *Sergeant Flynn* taken from the song of the same name, published in 1878 and in the public domain.

Chapter One

"You're like all the rest of them, goddammit!"

The shrill words penetrated thick billows of steam and rose in strident urgency over the rumble of the Shower Massage head that jetted scalding water onto J.C. Stonewall's broad muscular back. The pulsating liquid soothed the tough scar tissue that latticed his sun-browned flesh. His ears suffered, though, as the tirade continued.

"Naughty little boys, playing at being soldiers in your baggy green pants, grubby hands clutching ugly phallic symbol guns."

Stonewall turned off the shower. "God, guns and guts, baby. That's what made America. You'd do well to remember that."

"That's disgusting. It's nothing but a mindless slogan to justify oppression and exploitation Yankee-style." Stonewall began to towel himself while Karol's voice quality changed, took on a throaty, wheedling tone. "You could be different than the others, Stonewall. All you must do is grow up. It takes a real man to resist the seductive lure of the *machismo* mystique that surrounds professional soldiering. Can't you see it? Those long, hard, iron gun barrels are nothing but a cook substitute, something to compensate for sexual inadequacy."

"Bullshit!" Stonewall snapped. "I've never heard any complaints from you about that department. You aren't casting around for a replacement, are you?

7

You've set the scene for it well enough. Complete with the obligatory Lib Lady tantrum, filled with self-justifying cliches and blistering epithets. I expected better from you, Karol, really I did."

He shouldn't be so hard on her, Stonewall realized with a resigned shrug. After all, Karol was only being herself; bitching her little liberal ass off. Naked, Stonewall stepped into the bedroom of his townhouse on Woodhaven Circle in Fayetteville, North Carolina. Karol stood, in all her bare-fleshed loveliness, beside the huge waterbed. Her long, bright locks hung in graceful waves to golden shoulders and her firm, young breasts rose, taut with anger. She hadn't moved from where he had left her when the phone call had sent him to the shower instead of into a third, delicious bout of languorous love-making. He had known Karol for a considerable time, the thought struck him.

Their part-time, live-in girlfriend arrangement had endured much longer than any previous semi-permanent attachments. Karol was a lawyer, and a good one. Usually she had her shit together better than this. She was bright, pertly attractive and a sexual innovation far too good to lose. But when any mention of politics or Stonewall's occupation as a soldier for hire came up, her brain turned off and control of her mouth descended to the gut level.

She couldn't help being what she was, Stonewall admitted to himself. Karol was one of that generation which had been propagandized and bullshitted almost from birth. Their brains had been turned to pudding by the fucking boob tube, then they'd been molded into conformist, lowest-common-denominator shit-heads by the fucking snot-nosed kids who masqueraded as teachers—many of whom, it had recently turned out, could not pass even a simple literacy test—and then

8

radicalized by the fucking Marxist asshole professors at the universities.

Stonewall firmly believed that liberals, leftists, weren't born, they were made. Manufactured in identical rows of regimented automatons who could be counted on to perform predictable knee-jerk responses to patent Marxist stimuli. No, Karol could not be held responsible for what she had become.

That didn't make it any easier to live around her, though, when she trotted out her favorite Red cliches; *fascist, racist,* and worst of all, *mercenary.* Stonewall held strong views on the latter. On a couple of occasions they had come close to the knock-down, drag-out stage over that word.

A mercenary, Stonewall insisted, would fight for anyone, any time, anywhere. On the other hand, he held principles above all other things. In essence, he hated commies. Any size, any sex, any color, communists, and their liberal fellow travelers, were like pestiferous crap, dripping from the diseased anus of the world-wide Marxist conspiracy. Once, there had been a time when young J.C., football star and hero of the Tyler, Texas High baseball team, had not cared what anyone thought or how they might be governed. That had been before a war in a place called Vietnam and a quiet village in Laos where the uncommitted Green Beret, Stonewall, had found love and peace . . . for a while.

Then the commies came. Little, slant-eyed, slope-headed followers of that asshole paragon of Marxist virtue, Ho Chi Mihn. They raped and mutilated his love, violated his beautiful Angelique in manners blatantly cruel and subtly inhuman. Then, sated on gore, they had departed, proudly flying their yellow-star banner.

It was the same flag that so-called anti-war

demonstrators of Karol's generation wrapped themselves in and painted on their decrepit automobiles. With perfect knee-jerk reflex, those brainwashed bastards had marched in lock-step behind the filthy North Vietnamese rag to the beat of that traitorous Hollywood bitch's drum. All of it had left Stonewall a changed man, dedicated to awful and all-encompassing vengeance. He would not stop, he vowed, until he waded hip-deep in communist blood.

"Where is it now? Which helpless, peace-loving, emerging nation's government are you and your blood-soaked mercenary friends going to disrupt this time?"

Oh, Christ! She's still at it. The heated words interrupted Stonewall's reverie. "From what I gathered, it's . . . Libya."

"Ah, shit! I might have known. Isn't it enough that our fascist, warmonger president allowed those innocent Libyan pilots to be murdered while he slept in total ignorance?"

"I'm curious. Where did you get that pat, made-in-Moscow version of the incident? It had to be off the idiot box. Don't tell me, let me guess. I know! It couldn't be anyone but Dangerous Dan the Red-lovin' Man, right? Did it ever occur to you that if it hadn't been for the spineless policies of that gutless-wonder bunny basher and his redneck, retard brother, it wouldn't have been necessary to get your leftist buddy, Qaddafi's attention in such a way? No, I suppose not."

"Boy! You're really off into this one, aren't you?"

"Come on, Karol. You know what I do for a living. You've always known. Can't you let it go—just this once? I make the assholes bleed so there can be one place in this rotten world where you are free to spout your idiotic liberal garbage without fear of the secret police and a knock on the door at midnight. If that isn't good enough for you, then fuck off."

Karol snatched up a glass ashtray from the bedside table and hurled it at Stonewall, who easily evaded it with a slight sideways movement of his head. "I might just do that!" she yelled. "Don't expect to find me here when you come back from this blood-bath. God, you're hopeless."

Stonewall roared with laughter. His mouth opened wide, head thrown back. He felt the anger and irritation drain from his tense body and a warmth spread from his loins. "You know, there's nothing more beautiful than an angry, naked woman. Come here and kiss me."

Karol did.

"Mummm. I like that," she told him in a breathless pant.

"I know something else you like."

"And I've found it," Karol chortled deep in her throat while her slim, tapered fingers encircled Stonewall's rigidly erect penis. She expertly guided the throbbing tip to her moist mound that palpitated with expectancy. "Do we have time for a quickie?"

"There's always time on Stonewall's clock," he told her.

"Get those yellow feathers out of the corner of your mouth," Hank Polanski, a burly, giant of an ex-sergeant major greeted Stonewall thirty minutes later from a booth at the rear of Sol's Place, one of the more infamous watering holes on Combat Alley in Fayetteville.

"What are you talking about, Polanski?"

"You look like the proverbial cat who swallowed the legendary canary. Tell me, Cap'n, did you get a little nooner?"

"Naw. Not this kid. I got a morner."

"A morner? What's that, Cap?" Theodopholis Levi inquired, his obsidian eyes sparkling mischievously in his narrow, black face.

"That's a nooner, only sooner."

"Laugh?" Polanski grumped. "First time I heard

that I laughed so hard I thought I'd kick the slats outta my cradle. Our main man ain't here yet. Sit down and have some suds." Polanski poured beer from the communal pitcher, one of two that sat on the table. For his own part, he didn't believe in wasting time with a mug.

Easing himself into the booth, Stonewall glanced around the large bar room. A wide-spread, green camouflage-pattern parachute canopy hung from the ceiling. The wall behind the beer taps was covered with framed eight-by-ten glossy photographs. In each the subject was the same. Grim-faced, steel-helmeted youngsters stood spraddle-legged, hunched over in their harness, from which was suspended their backpack and chest reserve parachute deployment bags, field gear and primary weapon.

Their many-pocketed jump pants bulged with other equipment and were neatly bloused at the top of their shiny paratrooper boots. Uniformly pale of complexion, these boys-fashioned-into-men had penned flamboyant phrases and ribald verses along with the inevitable autographs and dates that commemorated their Cherry Jump, that first hitting of the blast with their unit, following the mandatory five school jumps. With a twinge of nostalgia, Stonewall recalled that he, too, had once had his picture up there.

"Unh-oh, that could be our boy," Levi indicated with a nod toward an obvious outsider who had wandered through the open front door.

The stranger made his way directly to the booth where the three soldiers of fortune waited. "Mr. Stonewall? I'm Ted Swink. Trojan sent me."

"Sit, Swink. What's this all about?"

Ted Swink looked with distaste at the foam-flecked pitchers and the amber brew before each man. "Can we get something to eat here? This is a serious matter."

"And you don't want to talk to a bunch of drunks,

right?" Polanski gave Trojan's representative a nasty sneer over the rim of his upraised pitcher. He drank deeply.

"You can eat here if you're immune to ptomaine," Stonewall suggested. "For my own taste, I'd rather we went to Odell's Barbecue or Harvey's Steak House. I picked this place because we can talk here undisturbed. Sol's in the back countin' his money and we serve ourselves on the beer." He produced a silver pint flask from his hip pocket and took a deep draught of scotch.

"Me, I prefer scotch. Want a toke?"

"No, thanks. You are aware of the confidentiality of this matter? It is highly sensitive."

Stonewall took time to extract a Kent from a crumpled pack and touch its tip with a silver-plated Zippo. "So give. From what Trojan told me on the phone, I gather the destination is in North Africa."

"Right, Mr. Stonewall. Libya to be exact."

"It's about time someone took a swig at that terrorist-loving son of a bitch, Qaddafi," Stonewall growled. "What's the nature of the operation?"

Swink opened his attache case and produced a slim file folder that contained three black-and-white glossy photos. "Three men, all of them known to you gentlemen, have gone over to the other side. They work for Qaddafi now. The first," he passed around a picture of a ruggedly handsome man in his early to mid- forties, "is Marc Tolliver."

"Former major with the Forces, CO of a B Team, right?"

"Correct, Mr. Stonewall."

"That mother-fucker, 'El Che,' " Theo Levi growled.

"You're right, Mr. Levi. Trojan indicated you had a more complete knowledge of the subject."

"I was a sergeant major, Swink. Call me Levi or Theo, not Mister."

"Yes, of course . . . ah, Theo. Would you fill us in?"

"If Marc Tolliver wasn't a fuckin' Red from the gate, I'll kiss your white ass. How he kept his clearances and stayed in the Forces so long, I'll never know. He was some sort of fanatic. I was his first shirt for a while. He overtrained, gave too much leave, too often and nit-picked the troops on inspections. A rule-book soldier and a guardhouse lawyer all rolled into one. He wasn't much of a fighter, but one hell of an administrator. Nothin', but nothin' was ever out of place in the property book, or the company journal, two-oh-ones all up to date on every man. She-it, that was one fussy dude. And spoutin' off at any occasion about what a super guerrilla fighter Mao was and how Che Guevara was the ideal example of the modern revolutionary."

"Can you get inside his head a little for us?" Swink urged.

Levi frowned, a gap-toothed, white grimace accompanied his efforts to conjure an image. "I'd say kinky, man, from the gate. I remember one time, we was out by Loc Bihn, at this Sneaky Pete firebase built, oh, maybe a year before. Long about midnight, Charlie comes shittin' an' a gittin' across the dead zone, primed on *bahng* and rice wine. It got hot for a while, until I dragged some dead carcasses off the Claymore console and started bangin' off the big ones. All the while, ol' 'El Che' is cool as iced shit, aiming and tickin' off neat three round bursts, drops a man every time. Then, after the firefight got rolled up, we went out to try for a body cout. Here's the Major stumblin' over the tore-up ground with tears runnin' down his face. An' he keeps sayin' some crazy shit, like, 'Oh, you magnificent bastards. Why do we have to be on opposite sides?' " Levi shook his head in disgust at the memory.

"He didn't have both oars in the water, I tell you. To make matters worse, he was a vegetarian, a real food freak. It was all the time, organic this and organic that and don't eat that rotten poison. Now I'll admit Cee rations ain't exactly dinner at the Ritz, but you show me the time when hot garbage don't beat no garbage at all. So what if the sausage patties are made of ground pig assholes? Long as they wipe 'em first, I'll warm them on a machinegun barrel and gobble the whole can. Not ol' 'El Che,' though. Wouldn't touch any of it. He'd chop open the cans and bury all that stuff in the latrine before he'd let any of the rest of us have his share. Said he didn't want to contribute to the decay of our bodies. Crazy fucker, you ask me."

"What about this man?" Swink coolly inquired, handing Polanski another photo. It depicted a boyishly young, blank-expressioned face with watery blue eyes, curly blond hair, that hung lank over a round head that emphasized his cup-handle ears. His thin lips had a weak, effeminate set to them.

"Yeah. Barry the Bird. Howard Byrd," Polanski enlarged. "He went into the Company when he left the Forces. A nasty little rat if you want my opinion. Say, before we go further, wasn't there some scandal involving Tolliver?"

"Definitely," Swink provided. "Marc Tolliver had been reassigned back Stateside, to the Command and General Staff School, as a matter of fact. Right at that time, the service club scheme broke. It seems Tolliver was, how do you say it, right up to his greedy ears in the group from the officer corps who provided cover and protection for the sergeants who operated the scam. There was talk of a court martial at the time, but Tolliver was allowed to resign quietly. Six months later he turns up in the CIA."

"No shit?" Levi barked, surprised. "Don't they check out anybody they recruit?"

15

"Tolliver had one particular specialty they badly needed. He was an expert on Middle-Eastern language and culture. And, outside the club scandal, he had a spotless record with the army. Anyway, this time they blew it big. Tollliver wasn't inside Libya two months before he defected to Qaddafi's secret police, the *shurtah*. Trojan's in-country sources reported that Tolliver was given a big welcome by the DGPI brass, in particular from Mustafa al Hawaadi, a Lieutenant Colonel in the Directorate General of Public Investigations, and the man in charge of the Libyan side of the project it will be your responsibility to terminate. More on that later, now let's get back to Howard Byrd."

"There's not a lot to tell," Polanski began, his big frame hunched over the beer-wet table. "He was a slimey little fucker when I had him in an outfit out Hung Mihn way. He was a complete missfit for Special Forces. A born snitch, if you know what I mean. He cheated at cards and when some·of my poker playin' buddies caught him and broke two fingers to teach him a lesson, he informed on them. Big photographer type, though. A lot of guys were. I heard not long ago that he got cashiered out of the Company when they discovered he had provided information to the Cong, the NVA and had been a source for Hanoi Jane and her shitheel crew here in the States. Not surprising, the little prick."

"Again, correct. Mr. Byrd was dismissed from his position with the Agency six months ago. Three weeks later he surfaced in Libya, alongside Marc Tolliver. Here's the final man Trojan wants you to interest yourselves in."

Stonewall pursed his lips and emitted a thin whistle. "Pete Guterrez. I'll be damned. He was a psy-ops specialist and damned good at it. He's another one that went with the Company."

16

"Yes. And stayed with the CIA for seven years, until the last day when he went over to the Libyans."

"What the hell are three ex-Green Beanies doing playing games with Maummar Qaddafi?" Stonewall asked Swink.

"They are working for al Hawaadi on a project called *Noor Mawt.*"

"Death Light," Polanski translated. "Don't tell us that Qaddafi is into some ray gun science fiction crap."

"Not at all. Colonel Qaddafi has given his personal support to *Noor Mawt,* a project to develop atomic weapons and delivery systems so they can be used against the United States."

"Son of a bitch!" Amazement flattened Polanski's broad, Polish features.

"Why doesn't the government do something about it?" Stonewall demanded, his level gray gaze boring into Ted Swink's impassive face.

"Simple. They aren't aware of it yet. Trojan only recently received verification of *Noor Mawt.* It's highly secret and carefully guarded. Trojan wants you, and whatever associates you want to take along, to locate the hidden factory and stockpile and destroy them. You are also to, ah, terminate the three American turncoats."

"That still sounds like a job for the Company. It's their dirtied drawers, why don't they clean up after themselves?"

"Precisely the reaction Trojan predicted for you. Why you and not them? It is Trojan's studied opinion, one in which I concur, that were the President to be informed of this and decide to take direct action, word might leak out, which it would. Then all the liberals in the Congress and Senate would turn it into a *cause célèbre* to intensify their attacks on the administration. That's something the country can ill afford."

17

"Yeah," Stonewall agreed. "Especially that friend of every Red regime, the Massachusetts Midnight Driver. He'd have a ball with it." A concentrated frown creased his broad brow, drawing down the curl-accentuated widow's peak of white hair.

Crazy. Trojan had finally flipped all the way out. All he wants is for us to locate an atomic bomb factory, wipe it out and frag three American traitors. But, what the hell? It provides an opportunity to take a swing at that arrogant, Marxist bastard Qaddafi, who has the same political outlook and could be an identical twin of the Koolaid Kid from Jonestown. He has the same moral scruples, too, Stonewall added as an afterthought. A broad smile washed away all sign of concern.

"Sure. Why not? Tell Trojan I'll get right on it."

"How many associates will you take with you?"

"I'll need any in-country assistance I can get. And I'll take Polanski with me."

"Hey! No fair. He's been gettin' the lion's share lately," Theo Levi protested.

"There's good reason, Theo. Hank speaks flawless Arabic and even can manage a little of the Berber dialect. He also speaks Italian, which is the closest thing to a second language in Libya. Besides, that amorous blacksnake of yours would get us in trouble among the locals. You know how strict the Moslems are about their women."

"Don't I just. Still, Cap'n, I gotta file a grievance."

"Take it up with the chaplain." Stonewall turned to Swink. "The usual financial arrangements?"

"Yes, plus an extra ten thousand bonus to all hands if you pull it off without setting off a nuclear blast."

"Shit. If we do that, won't be anyone collecting his pay," Polanski opined.

"I'll dictate a list of supplies I'll want to take in. How do we travel, by the way?"

"Your associate here will go to Frankfurt and on to Cairo, while you take a round-about route through Mexico City, Madrid and Cairo. You leave tomorrow, Saturday, Mr. Polanski two days later from New York."

"Sounds good. Now, I have a lot to do." Stonewall rose and strode purposefully from the saloon. Hot damn! More commie blood to spill, more guts to tear out. He could hardly wait.

"Maybelle," the gray-haired soldier of fortune spoke the single word into a telephone handset.

"That means you're going out again," Maybelle Anderson interrupted. "When are y'all goin' to get tired of riskin' your neck, honey?"

Stonewall let a grin break the hard line of his mouth before answering. Maybelle, a mountain of managerial efficiency, had brought a semblance of order to the contract soldier's operation. Short, prematurely white and extremely fond of chocolate, a widow for a shade over five years, she tried to play mother to the thirty-four-year-old Stonewall . . . a role her southern upbringing and childless life savored. Stonewall appreciated her efforts, if not her methods. In keeping with his position as CO and hers as "company scolder," he made his answers brisk.

"When I run out of Reds. Yes, Trojan has another one for me. Libya this time. Would you prepare the usual 'In the event of my death,' notices for the bankers and make sure there's an update on the list of my personal property and how it is to be distributed? We don't need to handle the airline tickets this time. Trojan has already taken care of it."

"Are you takin' that onery little black cat with you?"

"No, Maybelle. Polanski again. Call Lufthansa in the Big Apple and verify his reservations for Monday

19

morning, New York to Frankfurt, to Cairo. I'll see you when we get back."

"I tell you, honey, one of these times you're not goin' to come back. And then what will I do?"

"Don't worry. The bullet hasn't been made yet with my name on it."

"I'm not so sure of that."

Stonewall thought he detected the sound of gathering tears in Maybelle's forlorn words. He hung up and left the phone booth. What a hell of an assignment for Trojan to come up with, he thought once more. With Libyan trained terrorists still poised to assassinate top American officials, the Texas oil millionaire couldn't pick a worse time to kick Qaddafi's ass again.

Could be that this time Maybelle was right.

Chapter Two

"*¡Atención! Aeromexico anunciar* . . ." A soft, pleasing female voice continued announcing airline arrivals over the public address system in the spacious transient lounge of the Mexico City airport. At eleven-thirty, Stonewall still had half an hour before his noon departure on Iberia Airlines for Madrid. Seated beside him at the bar was Ted Swink, who sipped apprehensively at a Tom Collins while the soldier of fortune took his three-dollar-a-shot scotch over the rocks.

"I'd like to be going with you," Swink announced, surprising Stonewall with the intensity of his sincerity. "I've not been involved in field work for three years now. Trojan has kept me at a desk since I took a bad one in the gut."

"Oh?" The gray-haired Texan's tone invited further comment, though he personally disliked and distrusted confidentialities between those in his line of work.

Swink nodded toward the frost-beaded glass. "I'm not supposed to take any alcohol. I've only got half a stomach. Trojan figured that the frequent changes of diet, bad water, all of that would affect my performance, though he kept me on the payroll." Swink bent his face into a grimace that resembled an almost shy smile. "He claims it's because my administrative abilities keep the ball rolling. To be brutally honest, I think he's letting emotion get in the way of sound judgement."

"How's that?"

"The slug I caught was meant for him."

"Well, I'll be damned. That's one about Trojan I

hadn't heard before."

"It embarrasses me to talk about it. I'm sure it does him, too. You see, it didn't happen in any exotic foreign country. It was in New York, of all places."

"Yeah. Ain't gun control wonderful. Look, if it makes you uncomfortable, there's no need to go into a long explanation."

"Oh, I'm not going to bore you with all the gory details. You have your itinerary? One of Eric's men will meet you in Cairo. From there on it's up to whatever he has put together."

Stonewall polished off his scotch in a long, smooth swallow. "I'd better get to the boarding area."

"Right. Ah, good luck, Mr. Stonewall."

"Thanks."

Twenty minutes later the big Iberia 747 braked slightly and then spun on one set of wheels to line up with the center of the runway. The big jet engines thundered to max power and the eager bird leaped forward. Stonewall's first class accommodations provided him a wide, comfortable lounge chair right off the upper level bar. An olive-skinned, painfully handsome, Latin-lover type flight attendant had been paired with the trim-waisted lovely who had checked Stonewall's boarding pass. He made himself more obnoxious by rolling, big, brown marble eyes at all the female passengers and fussing over their carry-on luggage. Stonewall contented himself by peering intently out at the dirty-white ribbon of runway until it disappeared, to be replaced by a startlingly clear view of Popocatapatl. When the pilot completed his climbout and turned off the seat belt and no smoking signs, the soldier for hire looed up into the inviting heart-shaped face of the doll-like Spanish hostess.

"Would you care for a drink at your seat, *Señor?* Or you can go to the bar."

Stonewall came to his feet and found his chest only inches from the firm young breasts. "Here would be fine, if only you could join me."

The girl flashed him a warm, very unprofessional smile. "That would cost me my job *Señor*. Though it might be worth it," she added in Spanish. A small gold badge gave her name as Elena Carvajal.

A command of border lingo put an instant reply on Stonewall's lips. *"Seguro igualment. ¿Como sí, como no?"* Somehow, the tall, smiling soldier of fortune thought, 'Likewise I'm sure,' always came out sounding better in Spanish than English.

A musical titter escaped from behind the small hand she threw in front of her lips, while a delicate blush flamed her cheeks. "Oh, *Señor*, you speak Spanish," she responded in that language. "You are having fun with me, no?"

Stonewall's steady gray eyes bored intently into her sparkling black ones. "I'd certainly like to."

She excused herself and darted to the care of another passenger, giving the broad-shouldered American an inviting backward glance. Stonewall ambled to the bar.

"Scotch."

"*Sí, Señor*." The bartender poured, lingered. "This is your first trip to Spain?" he inquired.

"You could say that." Stonewall lighted a Kent.

"Ah, so beautiful a country. And the *señoritas* . . ." Expansive gestures clearly illustrated the barman's expertise in the field of feminine excellence. "You must go to the *Prado* in Madrid, about sixteen or seventeen hours for the *Paseo*."

He kissed his fingertips in an abandon of Iberian appreciation. "*¡Aye de mí!* those beautiful behinds wiggling this way and that. In all the world it is without comparison. The wines are nearly as magnificent as the view. All of Spain's finest; sherry, port, Madeira. And the oysters! I tell you, *Señor*, they are small and delicate as a baby's fist and so sweet you can savor them even when dipped in the manliest *salsa* ever devised. It used to be that you got them free with a bottle of wine. Now," he gave a resigned shrug, "with the inflation, there is a charge, but worth every *centimo*."

Amused, Stonewall signaled for another drink and fired up a second Kent. "Do you also work for the tourist bureau?"

"What is so strange, *Señor*? In me you see a man completely in love with his country."

"I gathered that. Nice talking with you." The soldier of fortune strolled back to his seat.

Munchies came around and Stonewall consumed more scotch. In late afternoon the flight attendants circulated large trays of canapés and hot hors d'oeuvres. Night time blanketed the Atlantic and, feeling the effect of the scotch, Stonewall looked forward to dinner. When it came, a masterful *paella* loaded with bits of chicken and fat, succulent shrimp, he felt compensated for his patience. After the movie, in Spanish without subtitles, the cabin crew began to arrange curtain partitions that made pairs and single seats into roomettes.

Stonewall finished a final scotch and had only eased himself back in his reclining seat when Elena Carvajan parted the hanging drape and slipped into the small space between the aisle and Stonewall's chair. For a moment she held one small finger to her lips to signal silence, then began to wriggle her way out of her uniform jacket. Stonewall came to his feet, filled with a wondrous disbelief. Elena flowed into his arms and pressed her firm, young body tightly against the growing bulk of his rapidly rising erection.

"Aaah, you are more man that any I have ever known. For this it is indeed worth the risk." Her almond-shaped, gloss-coated nails reached above the fiery highlights of her black-sheened hair and pressed the switch plate of the overhead light.

Elena left two hours before daylight. She dressed without a word, kissed Stonewall's sleeping lips and faded into the darkened aircraft. To the prematurely gray soldier for hire, who felt sated and somewhat smugly self-assured, sunrise over the Atlantic put on a show of special beauty. Delicate pinks and bold golds tinted the dark purple canopy and pushed back the stars with the gentlest baby blue. They would be in Madrid at eight-thirty. Stonewall thought over what the bartender had told him.

With a four-hour layover, if he could not talk the sweet-natured Elena into a rematch, he would take in the view around the Prado. Although mid-morning would not be nearly so spectacular as the ritual late afternoon *Paseo,* a little judicious girl-watching always proved to be a good way of spending time. Stonewall passed up breakfast and drank three cups of strong, sweet coffee, laced with rich Cavalos brandy. The flight arrived five minutes early.

With his luggage checked through to Cairo, Stonewall had no trouble clearing customs. Elena had been remote and only officially cordial to him. Her refusal of his offer had been firm and final. He caught a taxi and rode into the center of the magnificent city, a careful and intriguing mixture of the ancient and modern. Stonewall indicated a clean, sun-drenched sidewalk cafe, paid his driver with a handful of *pesetas* and settled in at a small, round marble-topped wire-leg table. A waiter in the traditional white shirt, black trousers and white half-apron tied around his waist, bowed obsequiously at Stonewall's side and hurried away with his order for Madeira and *ostiones.* A bevy of young women walked in his direction.

Not bad, Stonewall mused. Firm, roundly perfect bottoms wiggled and writhed inside tight-fitting skirts, providing ample visibility to the connoisseur. The wine and oysters arrived before another cluster of lovely office workers churned their way past Stonewall's observation point. He sipped deeply of the sweet, fruity libation and speared one of the shiny, slippery, gray-green sea creatures on a silver fork. A quick dip into a bowl of watery, reddish paste and he popsed the living mollusk into his mouth. Contrasting dark eyebrows crawled toward a white, receding hairline in pleased discovery.

He might have stocked a poor brand of scotch, but the Iberian bartender had definitely been right about everything else. The girls were most watchable, the wine delightful to taste, the oysters exciting in flavor and the sauce definitely torrid. A pair of healthfully glowing, cleanly scrubbed beauties, properly cupped and curved, undulated by. If the *Paseo* offered greater delicacies than those he now enjoyed, Stonewall mused, it would not be a fit engagement for a coronary patient. Stonewall readied his senses for more gratifying assaults.

A car pulled to the curb and three men got out. They bulked around Stonewall's table. "You are *Señor* Stonewall?" a statement, not a question.

J. C. Stonewall took a look at the fat bulk of a suppressor attached to the muzzle of a blackly gleaming automatic pistol. The man who held it, big for a Spaniard, kept the slitted lips of the end-wipe pointed directly at Stonewall's forehead. A Soveiet made Makarov, Stonewall judged from its shape.

"You will come with us, get into that car and make no noise. If you attempt to escape or draw attention to us, you will die right here. Now, move."

Stonewall placed both hands, palms down, on the tiny tabletop and thrust himself upward with cautious slowness. "Give a guy a break, will ya? I haven't finished watching the pretty girls."

"Bourgeois, capitalist pig!" one burly thug hissed in Stonewall's right ear. "You insult the womanhood of Spain."

"Shut up, Alfonso. To the car, Mr. Stonewall," the leader snapped.

Shit. Grabbed by a trio of commie pricks in the middle of the Spanish capital. It is a long way to Libya. If he couldn't do better than this, Stonewall thought cynically, he'd better hang up his combat boots and buy a cane. If this present collection of creeps let him live long enough, that is.

Without further comment, Stonewall complied.

Alfonso hurried ahead and opened the rear door of a four passenger Renault. "Inside, quickly," the man with the gun ordered.

Stonewall slid across the cheap vinyl seat and his oversized abductor wedged his bulk in after. Alfonso and the other flunky took the front.

"Where do we take him, Comrade Miguel?" Alfonso inquired.

"Have Hector drive us to the farm."

"Yes, Comrade."

When the tiny French car sped from the curb, Stonewall turned to study his captor. "Who sent you to get me?" he inquired in Mexican-accented Spanish.

Thick lips opened in a wet, red circle. "The name wouldn't mean anything to you, Mr. Stonewall. Sit back and enjoy the ride."

What could he do, Stonewall wondered. The man had him by a hundred pounds, not to mention to tidy Makarov held competently in his right hand, away from the soldier of fortune. He needed a distraction and his only choice seemed to be to wait until one came along.

"How can I do that under the circumstances?"

Miguel's thick left hand came up and brushed back the front edge of a blue Basque beret. "Why is that?"

"If the driver didn't know where we were going, I figure this will be a one way trip for me."

"My instructions did not include providing you with unessential information. Really, Mr. Stonewall, this will all go a lot easier if you relax and accept the inevitable."

Stonewall twisted even further on the seat and let his gaze appear to wander beyond the sidewindow to the streets of Madrid. Suddenly he snapped his fingers and leaned forward, close to the back of the driver's head.

"Hey, I didn't leave any money for my bill."

"Never mind that," Miguel told him. "The manager will take it out of the waiter's pay and that will make him hate Americans and the bourgeois shop owners even more. Now sit back."

Once more Stonewall complied with no show of resistance. Miguel had watched his every move, but the Makarov did not track along with him. Apparently the hefty communist agent thought he had complete command. Stonewall fished in his shirt pocket for the crumpled pack of Kents.

"Do you mind if I smoke?"

"For the nerves, eh?"

"Something like that," Stonewall agreed.

"You might as well, I suppose. Another of life's pleasures that you should enjoy to the fullest at this time," Miguel observed while the soldier for hire took a slender white cylinder from the package, straightened it and dug into one trouser pocket for his lighter.

A nervous smile forced its way onto Stonewall's face while he fumbled with the Zippo. He managed to open the hinged top and flicked the flint wheel. The fluid fumes ignited in an orange blossom. With a sudden, violent snap of the wrist, Stonewall threw the flaming lighter at Miguel's face.

In the same instant he powered a *mae geri keage* front snap kick into the vulnerable spot below Miguel's rib cage. His left hand flew forward and slapped Miguel's Russian-made automatic toward the roof. The suppressor coughed once before the tip of Stonewall's shoe drove into Miguel's solar plexus.

"Unnngph!" Sour air rushed from Miguel's mouth. His eyes bulged and his face flushed scarlet. Already Stonewall had one hand on the gun.

Only partly conscious, Miguel struggled to retain control of the Makarov. He lashed out with his big left fist and caught Stonewall a ringing blow along side of his head. The American continued to move, though, grappling to keep the deadly pistol pointed away from him. He balled his right hand, second knuckle protruding and smashed it into Miguel's left eye. Immediately the Spaniard's grip loosed on the Soviet 9mm auto. Stonewall snatched it up and whirled in time to barely escape a vicious slash from the knife on Alfonso's hand. Stonewall squeezed the trigger, aiming blindly.

The Makarov burped quietly.

Blood squirted from Alfonso's ears and the back of his head splashed against the windshield. He catapulted backward and fell in a tangled heap on the floor of the speeding vehicle. With a grunt of rage and frustration, Miguel got back into the fight.

Miguel grabbed Stonewall from behind, wrapped his big arms around the American's chest and began to crush him in a powerful bear hug. Stonewall whipped his right arm back in a *yoko hiji ate* side elbow strike that connected with Miguel's right temple.

Fragile bone cracked under the force. Miguel's eyes glazed and his formidable bear hug became a gentle lover's embrace. Stonewall turned then and shot Miguel twice in the chest. At last he could direct his attention to the driver.

All through the fight, in panic and confusion, Hector had been careening along a narrow street in the old quarter of Madrid. He hurtled around another corner a moment before the cold metal of the Makarov's silencer pressed against his head, behind his right ear.

"If you have any sense, Hector," Stonewall spoke in soft Spanish, "you'll stop at the nearest phone booth."

Two minutes later, the terrified young communist drew up beside a telephone kiosk. The Russian pistol still in one hand, Stonewall pulled the door latch and climbed out, eyes on the driver. Hector made a foolishly brave, fatal mistake.

When he believed Stonewall could no longer clearly see what he did, Hector shoved his left hand into the map pocket on the driver's door. He came out with a small M1950, 7.65 mm Czech pistol. He swung toward where he believed Stonewall would be, near the rear of the car, only to discover that the fast-moving, deadly American stood behind him at the open sidewindow.

"You commies are all such dumb fucks," Stonewall told Hector. "Oh, and another thing. Did I get around to telling you that Abraham Lincoln Brigade sucks." He shot the startled young Spanish communist three times in the forehead.

"That's right, I'm in a pile of very deep shit. Can you get out here right away?"

Halfway across Madrid from the phone booth Stonewall used to reach Trojan's office in the capital, Jerry Davis, the Iberian expert for Trojan's covert operations listened with a pained expression on his rough, pirate's visage. "Gawdamn, Stonewall, how'd y'all manage to get grabbed like that, no more'n an hour in the country?"

"You tell me. Just get here, okay? I've got a plane to catch for Cairo in a little under two hours."

"Okay. I'll come personally."

Ten minutes later, Jerry Davis pulled the black Mercedes to a stop behind the car full of corpses. *"Jesus!"* You sure made a mess in there, Stonewall."

"I didn't have time to be neat, just positive. Can you dispose of the bodies?"

"Sure. Brought along just the guy to do it, too. Raul."

A thin, nervous looking young *gitano* climbed from the Mercedes. In rapid Spanish, Davis gave instructions on the disposal of the corpses. When he completed his orders he turned to Stonewall.

"First, we'll check the bodies for any papers."

"You expect to find much?"

"Not really." The grisly task took only a few seconds. Grinning, Jerry Davis extended a wallet in one hand. "I thought I recognized that big one in the back seat. Miguel Flores del Campo Suerte. He and these other two are members of *Rejoño Rojo*, the Red Spear communist terrorist group. It's the biggest and worst one in Spain right now."

"I'm still asking, how did they get on to me and why? They even had my name. Someone sent them, set me up for the kill. Who?"

"We'll get on it, naturally. I'll telex Trojan soon's I get back to the office. I'll have to spread around a few pesetas in the neighborhood here, insure no eyes took in what happened. What time's that flight of yours?"

"Twelve-forty-five."

"No sweat. How about lunch and a cold beer?"

"Make mine scotch and you've got a deal. Where do we eat?"

"I know this place out close to the airport. It's run by another Mississippi boy, like me. He does the best barbecue, Spanish-style, of course, of any I know."

"For that I'll even drink a beer. Let's go."

Chapter Three

The sun hung several notches above the horizon and the oppressive heat of mid-day radiated from the ground and walls of buildings when J. C. Stonewall went to retrieve his luggage and stand in line to clear customs in Cairo. His flight had arrived at *Mahsre* International at six-twenty-five local time and now, twenty minutes later, he still slowly shuffled forward, passport in hand, to receive his entry stamp and have the government officials paw through his possessions.

"Mr. Stonewall? If you will come this way please?"

The professional warrior looked to one side where a smiling, uniformed Egyptian and a slender young American stood beckoning him.

"I'm Chuck Nelson, from Tex-San Outfitters," the American informed Stonewall.

"Mr. Bach sent me down to speed things up for you."

"I like your timing. From the looks of it, I'd be here another half an hour."

"More like an hour." With the Egyptian customs man in the lead, Stonewall and Nelson walked to a narrow door, inset in the wall dividing the international arrivals area from the remainder of the airport. Beyond it was a small cubicle of an office. The official extended his hand.

"Omar Hassad Nuri at your service, sir. Your passport, please?"

Stonewall shook hands and surrendered his well-worn, dark blue covered document. A rubber stamp made an imprint on the proper page. Nuri returned it and spoke again.

"If you would open your bag? A mere formality, though necessary, you understand?"

"Of course." Stonewall hefted his Val-Pac bag onto the desk and opened it. Nuri gave everything a cursory glance, then his hand darted out and rested momentarily on the tough, cow-hide sheath of Stonewall's assegai.

"Interesting. You bring African artifacts into Africa."

A smile flickered on Stonewall's lips. "It does wonders to discourage muggers."

"Mug . . . ? I'm afraid I do not understand."

"An inside joke," Chuck Nelson inserted. "Muggers are a type of cowardly criminal in America. They only prey on people they are sure can't resist them."

"I see. Interesting." Nuri's hand touched the assegai again. "What is it you do for Tex-San, Mr. Stonewall?"

"I'm a photographer," Stonewall responded at the same time Nelson spoke.

"He's a surveyor."

Was it really only ten percent who didn't get the word? Stonewall hastened to fill the sudden gap in conversation. "I do photographic surveys of likely areas for archeological digs."

"Do you encounter many, ah, muggers on your expeditions?" Nuri's question had dripped skepticism, though he closed the Val-Pac and kept his face impassive. "Welcome to Egypt, Mr. Stonewall."

"Ah . . . thank you, Mr. Nuri."

Outside the terminal, Nelson directed Stonewall to a desert-buff colored Land Rover. He took the wheel. When they left the parking lot, an ancient, battered VW bug pulled into line three cars behind them.

"Sorry about the screw-up back there. I really thought the cover you were using in Egypt was as a surveyor.'

33

"No sweat. We got away with it and I'm not going to be here that long. I was told to claim to be a photographer." Stonewall tapped a Kent on the crystal of his Rollex and stuck it in the corner of his mouth. "Do you have any scotch at the office?"

"A little. The price is outrageous here, being a Moselm country. Particularly since the British left so long ago." .

"All I need is a couple good belts."

After the third turn in the twisting streets of Cairo, Stonewall satisfied his suspicion. The VW bug had hung on their tail all the way. Someone had been on his ass from the start, first Madrid and now here. Would there be another attempt to kill him? He didn't mention the clumsy surveillance to Nelson. If he didn't tumble to it, tough shit. The Tex-San office building had a ground level parking garage. When they turned in, the VW sped on by.

On the third, and highest, floor, Nelson led Stonewall through a doorway into Eric Bach's private office. The slightly built, dark-haired man looked up at his visitor through gold wire-rimmed glasses.

"Well, Stonewall, I haven't seen you in a long time."

"Not since you were teaching martial arts to the Aussies."

"A lot has happened since then. Neither of us worked for Trojan at the time. Good to have you here. Ah, by the way, Trojan sent along a little gift for you. Said I should see you got it first thing." Eric produced a compact, brown-paper wrapped package from his desk drawer and slid it across the polished surface. Devoid of any clutter, the desktop, like the nearly bare office, reflected Bach's spartan tastes. Stonewall reached for the present.

"What do we have here?"

"I don't know. Trojan seemed sure you'd appreciate it, though."

Brown paper crackled loudly while Stonewall used a penknife to slit the heavy strapping tape fastenings and unwind the package. Inside he discovered a small magnesium-alloy case. He released the catches and opened the lid. His eyebrows climbed his forehead.

"It's pretty, but what is it?"

Eric had come around his desk and looked on over Stonewall's shoulder. "That's a Sidewinder submachine gun. The best there is."

Lips turned down in disapproval, Stonewall pushed the box away from him. "What's that for? All I need is my Uzi."

"It's more versatile than a Uzi. It converts from forty-five ACP to nine millimeter. And it combines all the best features of the Uzi and Ingram, with a revolving receiver that lets you swing the magazine out of the way no matter how you have to hold it."

Stonewall brightened. "Yeah, I've heard about that. I read a couple of articles on it by Chuck Taylor and another by some guy named Roberts. They seemed impressed by it."

. "Rightly so," Eric advanced in his professorish, Wally Cox manner. "It has a three-stage progressive trigger to allow for single shot, three round burst and full auto. With the pistol grip and trigger far forward of the receiver and ejection port, it points like a handgun. The butt plate there pulls out into a telescoping metal stock for shoulder use, too."

Stonewall had drawn the revolutionary new firearm back to give it closer inspection. He lifted a long, fat cylinder from the pliable rubber foam interior. "This is some sort of suppressor but I don't recognize the make."

"McQueen, the man who created the Sidewinder, invented that, too," Eric explained. "It's a lot more efficient than a MAC and the closest thing to a true silencer you can find. He does custom work on pistols and rifles, also. What do you think now?"

"Well—maybe I should give it a try. After all, Trojan did make me a present of it."

"Fine. Then we'd better start making a list of what you want to take into Libya." Eric pressed a stud on his intercom.

"Yes?"

"Can you come in a minute, Patty?"

"Yes, Mr. Bach."

When the innerconnecting door opened, Stonewall, who had been covertly admiring the Sidewinder, stopped his examination and merely stared. The young woman who entered had all the energetic ingenue vitality of Karol and the vivacious, blatant sexuality of Elene Carvajal, plus the apparent positive features of several other women Stonewall had known. She had a pixie face, surrounded by soft, dark auburn hair, cut short in a feathery style long out of date, but the most suited to her distribution of wide-set, deep green eyes aglow with a child-like innocence, pert nose and small, though generous and smiling mouth. She walked with a womanly grace that belied her appearance of chaste naivete. She stopped beside Eric's desk, poised, steno pad in hand.

"Stonewall, this is Patricia Sayers, my assistant and personal secretary."

"How do you do, Mr. Stonewall?"

The battle-scarred professional soldier grinned like a love-struck boy. "Better now that you're here."

"That sounds like a sincere compliment."

"It was meant to be."

"Shall we get down to business?" Eric Bach interrupted.

"Uh, sure, sure," Stonewall agreed. "Now, here's what I'll need. First off, a jeep, with a quarter-ton, two wheel trailer if possible."

"You'll have both waiting for you. You're going in by boat, so Trojan's man in Tripoli will arrange for that."

"Good, Eric. We'll need two forty-five autos and a couple of Browning Hi Powers if we need to convert to local ammo. An M-fourteen for Polanski and a Uzi . . . no, scratch that, I'll take the Sidewinder." Eric smiled a small, secret smile. "Say, fifteen hundred rounds of forty-five ACP, five hundred seven-six-two for the Fourteen, a case of white phosphorous grenades, three cases of fraggers. Can we get anti-tank weapons?"

"They're available in-country."

"Good. What about our assets? Will we be arming them?"

"Yes."

"How many men will I have?"

"Forty."

"Okay. AK's for them, forty count, five hundred rounds of seven-six-two Soviet for each."

"Why Kalasnikov's?"

"We don't exactly want to leave calling cards, do we?"

"Good thinking. What else?" Eric inquired.

"How do we stand on explosives?"

"At this point we don't know anything about the facility. Odds are it will be well built."

"Then let's go for a hundred pounds of plastique, Cee-Four if you can get it. Fifty pounds of RDX in blocks, another hundred pounds in satchel charges. A thousand foot reel of primer cord. A box of HDP primers and a case of electric det caps, about twenty time detonators. Three AN/PRC-Six radios."

"My God, are you planning on re-enacting World War Two?"

"Not exactly. If Qaddafi's boys have completed any nuclear weapons, we have to be able to destroy the bombs without them going critical. Since we're in the dark on that, it means we need a variety."

"Anything else?"

"Who all's coming out?"

"You, Polanski and Phil Nichols, Trojan's man in Libya."

"We'll need iron rations for, say six people for three days, then. For the exfiltration."

"Surely it won't take that long?"

"Again, we don't know. I don't like being this much in the dark, for any reason. We could be as far into the country as the Chad border, or Niger."

"This is a lot to haul in. Trojan says there's open season and no bag limit on Libyan troops. All of your heavy equipment can be acquired from them."

"Right. But the technical things we have to bring with us. That takes care of everything I can think of now. Didn't Trojan send you a duplicate list?"

"No. That's usual, though. We have to keep a low profile in this part of the world."

"Who pays the assets?"

Eric smiled. "The Tuaregs are strongly anti-communist. Since Qaddafi took over they've fared rather badly. From what I gather, the volunteers for this operation are glad for the opportunity to strike at their oppressors, so they'll do it free."

"Nothing like highly motivated troops." Stonewall rose. "If that's it, I want to get out of here, get a shower and take in the sights."

"Your hotel room is arranged," Patty Sayers injected. "At the National Palace on the Street of Coppersmiths."

"Fine." To Eric, Stonewall added, "I'll check in with you in the morning when Polanski arrives." He started for the door through which he had entered.

"Come this way, please, Mr. Stonewall," Patty instructed. Her eyes held a hint of unexpected promise and she arched her well-curved young body invitingly.

"And don't forget your present from Trojan."

Stonewall closed the metal case and lifted it by the handle. He followed Patty through the open portal. She paused beside her desk, a wet, haunting smile on her lips. Every gesture, each delightful line of her body telegraphed her interest in Stonewall as a man.

"Things don't really get started in Cairo until after nine at night," she offered.

"That gives me plenty of time to get refreshed. In any case, I'll need a guide." Stonewall made the invitation implicit in the soft, bass purr of his voice.

"I get off at eight."

"Good. What about drinks before dinner and . . . ?" He left it open.

"Sounds fine to me. We can have cocktails only in the hotels."

"How about my room?"

"You move fast, Stonewall."

"I didn't notice you dodging out of my way."

"Any girl who did that needs her head examined."

"Where shall I pick you up?"

"I'll meet you in your lobby."

Blowing sand from the Rebiana Sand Sea shrank the setting sun to a bloody tennis ball and diffused sickly crimson light along the horizon. Marc Tolliver slammed the half-full bottle of *Stolichnaya* vodka onto his desk top with a loud bang. His oddly smoky, opaque blue eyes smoldered with fury.

"Are you sure? Stonewall made it to Cairo? *J. C. Stonewall?*" He ran one blunt-fingered hand through his straight, jet-black hair, lingering a moment at one of identical streaks of pure white that sprouted, like emu plumes, from each temple.

"Yes, Comrade Tolliver. Colonel al Hawaadi assured me the message he received was correct."

"Tell Mustafa I want to see him here . . . now!"

The messenger bent low at the waist, his hand automatically darting to his breast and lips in the customary *salaam*, before he recovered his composure. "Yes *effen* . . . ah, yes, Comrade."

Shit! Marc Tolliver crushed the brittle plastic glass in one hard fist and threw it from him in frustrated anger. He took another container from a stack on one corner of the yellow-green, Russian made field desk and poured more vodka. Bad enough to have these turkeys calling him 'Comrade,' when in fact they couldn't stand half an hour against the Egpytian army no less. Now the Cong, that was another matter. Charlie had outsmarted and outfought the American forces in 'Nam at every turn. They had class, had to be admired. But to have these . . . these desert lice fuck up a plan he had devised was too much. Tolliver swallowed the clear liquor in a long, single gulp. He licked his thick, sensuous lips and reached for more *Stolichnaya*. A knock stopped him.

&° "Come in."

"You wanted to see me, Comrade Colonel Tolliver?"

"Yes, *Lt. Colonel* al Hawaadi. Precisely what happened? Stonewall was to have been eliminated in Madrid."

"Exactly. Our comrades in *El Rejoño Rojo* had detailed instructions, photographs. The man on board Stonewall's flight from Mexico City pointed him out as ordered. Then . . . then everything went wrong. This Stonewall killed all three men sent to apprehend him. How could that be? Do you know this man?"

"Yes, I know him, knew him," Tolliver corrected himself. "Even in Vietnam he was a mean, tough son of a bitch." He paused and let his eyes roam over the office. A large map of the eastern half of Libya occupied one wall, a black circle indicating the location of this secret base in the desert near the Zeltan oil fields. Inside this perimeter, another, red line distinguished the base itself. Between the two, he knew, jeep patrols, men on horseback and camel and four fat, sleekly deadly Soviet-made T-55 tanks patrolled day and night. Behind the well hidden, camouflaged fence worked twelve Soviet technicians and twenty Soviet-trained Libyan physicists.

At first, when Maummar Qaddafi had first approached him on the idea, Tolliver believed it would be a case of the blind leading the blind. He knew nothing about nuclear weapons, other than small tactical ones and how to employ them. The building he left to others. He felt certain that Libyan scientists, if they could be called that, knew even less. Reluctantly he had agreed and recruited two more Americans, whom he knew to harbor grudges against their homeland. They organized the site, supervised the necessary security and propaganda requirements. Then the Soviet technicians arrived.

He learned that no one needed a cyclotron anymore to make an atomic bomb. Somewhere someone had the needed materials. The Ruskies brought that with them and the work began almost immediately. Now they had succeeded.

A stockpile of slender, silvery cylinders had begun to stack up in the thick-walled, underground bunker. Then, from a man who sold reliable information Tolliver had learned that that lousy, super-fucking-patriot J. R. Kurin, oil millionaire and muddling damned interfering bastard had taken an interest in what he, Tolliver, Barry Byrd and Pete Guterrez were doing in Libya. Trojan he called himself and operated his own international intelligence network.

Well, fuck Jackson C. Kurin and fuck his number one hit man, do-gooder mercenary J. C. Stonewall. And fuck

Kurin's cat and his dog and his canary, too! They wouldn't shit in his messkit. When he pulled off this project, *Noor Mawt,* he'd have his own little empire secured right here in the Libyan desert. Who could tell? Even if the U.S. came over and started kicking ass and taking names, he might come out on top no matter which side won. First, though, he had to get rid of Stonewall.

His glance moved on, paused a second at a large metal rack bookshelf filled with field and technical manuals in English and Arabic. Small arms, machine guns, radio SOI's and SSI's. Field sanitation, desert survival, hell he had them all and, with the Bird's help and that of Pete Guterrez, he was building a cadre loyal to him and no one else. Given a little more time and it would be possible to challenge Qaddafi for control of the whole of fucking Libya. He returned his unreadable gaze to Mustafa al Hawaadi.

"Stonewall has to be stopped. Your people have one more chance, in Cairo. See that it succeeds. Even so, I have no choice but to report everything that has happened when I meet with Colonel Qaddafi tomorrow afternoon."

Al Hawaadi paled. Even though he worked for the powerful *shurtah,* the secret police of the Directorate General of Public Investigations, mention of the Libyan strongman's name and the reminder of how closely this American stood to the ruler, brought a cold, sick feeling to his stomach. He licked thin, harshly cruel lips with a narrow strip of pink tongue and brushed his long, spatulate fingers over the pencil line of black mustache that horizontally divided his upper lip.

"I will see to it, Comrade Colonel."

"You do that. By this time tomorrow, I want to hear that Stonewall is dead, dead, dead."

Stonewall splashed Johnnie Walker Black into a glass,

added three ice cubes and swirled the results a moment before sipping. When he left Eric Bach's phony archeological expedition outfitter's the VW bug had picked him up again. He wondered if it would be waiting when he and Patty went to dinner. He swallowed another gulp and mused over the assignment.

Wow! Qaddafi and the boys from Bum-fuck camelland. With Marc Tolliver thrown in for good measure. Qaddafi, darling of the United fucking Nations and palsy-walsy with the sickest, ugliest, bloodthirstiest terrorist of all times, pussy-lips Yassir Arafat. If the stripe-pants, slime ball assholes in Moscow Center-on-the-Hudson hadn't made bedfellows of those two their natural inclinations would have done so soon enough. Too bad he couldn't arrange to catch that pair of pricks together and cook off their atom bomb pile right under their balls! Marc Tolliver along with them. A professional bleeding-heart liberal in a Green Beret. A total missfit. Always blowing off about how splendid the Viet Cong were. Too bad Charlie didn't blow his whang off with one of their cute little Russian made landmines. Or fed him to the Pathet Lao instead of Angelique.

Angelique! The name, the sweet, loving face, the tender memories, ripped to shreds of sorrow and blind hatred, all boiled up again. Why? Why did he have to think of her now? Fuck you, Marc Tolliver! The Stonewall's coming to flatten your ass. Stonewall finished his scotch and started for the door.

"There you are, lovely lady," Stonewall greeted Patty when he found her sitting in the lobby, target of lustful, hungry leers from a dozen men of half that many nationalities.

"And there you are, you gorgeous male. I'm famished."

"Drink first, dine later, I always say. Shall we go?"

"Your room?"

"Like we'd planned. I have some Johnnie Black. Good enough?"

"Perfect. I have just the place to eat."

Upstairs, in Stonewall's room, he poured two glasses of scotch, added a splash of soda to Patty's and handed it to her. They lifted their arms in a casual toast.

"Here's to . . ." Stonewall offered.

"Us?"

"Why not?" Each drank, their eyes on the other, and set aside the tumblers. Stonewall drew Patty into his arms, his lips brushed her cheek. Pressed tightly to him, she felt the growing pressure in his loins.

"Take it easy, okay? The lady wants to be fed before she gets bred."

"Can't it be the other way around?"

"Are you always this horny?"

"No. Sometimes it's worse."

"You're hopeless, Stonewall. But I should have known. Horny little boys have been trying to get into my pants since I turned eight."

"Didn't any of them succeed?"

"Not until I reached twelve." Patty smiled, pressed a teasing finger to Stonewall's lips. "That's the past. I've learned a lot since then. You have no idea how rough it is on a gal in a place like this. Every local male thinks he's the ideal replacement for Valentino in *The Sheik*. Why, I've been prospositioned by kids, no bigger than this." She held out a hand to indicate a height mid-way between her full, bouncy breasts and cleverly curved hips.

"My dream . . ." Patty paused. "I've dreamed that someday Mr. Right would come along, a tall, broad shouldered, ruggedly handsome WASP type who would sweep me off my feet and take me away from all these swarthy, pint-sized lotharios."

"If I swept you off your feet right now, we'd wind up

in that bed over there."

Patty pressed a small, warm hand against his chest. "No. Let me have my pretty fantasy. I want to be wined, dined and carried away to my secluded bungalow in the suburbs."

Stonewall shrugged and reached for his jacket. "Shall we get started on that dream world?"

"Oh, I'd love to."

Dinner, at the *Ginayna al Rahsool*—the Garden of the Prophet—turned out to be an exotic, delightful mixture of Middle-Eastern dishes. Stonewall, who considered a Wendy's hamburger *haute cuisine*, found himself getting into the mood of the evening and enjoying every bite. He thought it wise not to mention to Patty the faded, battered Volkswagen that shadowed them to the restaurant.

The ubiquitous bug clung to them when they went to a small Egyptian night spot that featured belly dancers and incredibly thick, sweet coffee. It hung on until the taxi turned off into the cul de sac of *Sharia al Fill*. At the far end of the Street of Cork, a low, vine-shrouded cottage waited. A soft night light glowed in one window. Stonewall paid the driver and helped Patty onto the sidewalk.

"Welcome, sir, to my cozy abode," Patty intoned invitingly.

Inside, Patty tended to making tall, cool drinks while Stonewall removed his jacket and kicked off his shoes. He sipped gratefully on the scotch when Patty handed him a frosted glass. Patty stood on tiptoe and kissed him lightly on the lips, then disappeared into the single bedroom. When she returned she wore a sheer, sea-green pegnoir that matched her gold-flecked eyes and set off her dark russet hair.

"That's better," Stonewall commented approvingly. He began to undo the buttons of his shirt.

"Good Lord, you have a one-track mind, Stonewall. How about a little romance first."

" 'Love comes but once,' " Stonewall quoted, " 'The second time around.' Haven't you heard that old song?"

He removed his shirt and tossed it aside onto a low, chintz-covered sofa that stood in a soft pool of light from an abstract, ceramic base lamp. Patty's eyes widened at the sight of the many scars that latticed his body. She uttered a stifled little moan and propelled herself into his open, waiting arms.

Crushed close together, Stonewall felt the warmth of her body through the gauzy layer of material that separated them. He found her lips, moist and eager, and his tongue probed deeply into her mouth. Gently he lifted her and carried the luscious young woman into the bedroom. A tiny lamp on the nightstand shed scant light. A cynical smile briefly twisted Stonewall's lips when he saw that Patty had turned down the covers in anticipation.

She liked it that way. Oooh, did she like it! How precious, that warm hugeness, slowly plunging to fill her whole being with contentment. There had been others, she acknowledged, many of them, and he knew it too. Yet never one such as Stonewall. A kaleidoscope of sensual magnificence exploded behind her tightly clinched eyelids and the rhythm of her heart matched the pounding in his powerful chest that pressed against her. When at last, as it inevitably must, the soaring joy of their coupling comingled into glorious fulfillment, she cried out and raked his back with her nails.

"You were very sweet," she murmured when at last they were able to speak.

"And the dream?"

"Is reality."

Stonewall padded barefoot into the livingroom,

retrieved their drinks and his pack of Kents. When he retunred, he lighted one for her and a second for himself. They sipped and smoked and let silence be its own kind of conversation.

Patty ran her eyes over Stonewall's naked body and felt a stirring of new desire deep within her. Her hand glided to his thigh and slid upward, marveling that so scarred a body could feel so silky. For his own part, Stonewall reacted instantly. His erection swiftly burgeoned, a tall phallic lance eager for the quest. Patty's fingers deftly drew back his foreskin and guided that pulsing organ to a moist welcome.

A sudden sound, tinkling of falling glass, clattered on the floor, invaded the secret place into which their amorous exercises had taken them. Stonewall paused, listened. Patty returned to reality with a start.

"Wha-what is it?"

"Shsssh," the soldier of fortune cautioned.

Another faint clatter came from the kitchen, followed by the squeak of wooden table legs.

"Someone's in the house," Patty spoke the obvious.

Stonewall climbed from the bed and stepped into the deep shadows near the closet. Naked, the only weapons he had were his hands and the lamp on the bedside stand. Tensely he waited. A dark form appeared in the doorway, hesitated. Another joined it.

Two men leaped into the room, knives drawn and ready.

Chapter Four

With his left hand, Stonewall hurled his trousers into the face of the man farthest from him. His right snatched up the electric lamp and drove the bulb into the eyes of the nearest assailant.

"Yeeeow!" The bulb broke, sparks flew and the wounded, blood-streaming assassin jerked and convulsed in the deadly grip of electrical current. The would-be murderer dropped his knife. Immediately Stonewall released his hold on the fixture and scooped up the fallen blade.

Before the semi-conscious killer could sag to the floor, Stonewall plunged the curved *tulwahr* into his attacker's exposed abdomen and ripped upward. Blood and fluids splashed over his arm and Stonewall shoved the corpse away. He turned toward the second man, only to find him gone.

"Stay here," he commanded.

A quick search of the house verified the assassin had fled. Stonewall returned to the bedroom. To her credit, Patty had not made a sound throughout the encounter. Had it been Karol in the room, by now she would be bitching her head off about violating the civil rights of the killer or still consumed by hysterics.

"You did all right, kid," he told her with a glow of respect in his voice.

"If I could have reached my gun we'd have got the other one, too." She looked at the dead man. He wore typical native dress, his swarthy skin, pallid now in death, and hawk nose identified him as a local. "They picked the wrong house to burglarize," she commented.

"I'm not so sure of that," Stonewall called over his shoulder from the bathroom. He scrubbed the blood from his arm and came into the bedroom. He talked while he dressed.

"I've been followed since I got to Cairo. Before that, three Spanish commies jumped me in Madrid. This could be another attempt."

"Don't get paranoid over this," Patty cautioned. "These things happen all the time in Cairo. Three people on this block have been ripped off in the past month."

"We'll see," Stonewall replied, unconvinced. "Eric should be able to find out something about them."

Early the next morning, Stonewall left his hotel to pick up Polanski at the airport. Once more, the VW took up station three cars behind him. During what had been left of the night, Eric Bach had discovered the identity of the dead prowler. Achmed Maliq turned out to be a small-time burglar, sneak-thief and follower of a rabidly anti-government Moslem sect with strong ties to Iran and Libya. It could mean nothing, or a great deal. Stonewall bided his time, wending his way through heavy market-day traffic on his way to *Mahsre* International. A plan began to form in his mind.

Once he picked up the hulking Polak, they could do something about the tail. His foot slammed on the brake and his thumb gouged the horn button when a small boy, leading a heavily laden donkey, darted in front of the car Stonewall had borrowed from Eric Bach.

"*Hasib!*" Stonewall leaned from the window and hollered at the youngster in his limited command of the language.

"*You* look out," the laughing boy responded. He made an obscene gesture and disappeared into the swirling throng.

Twenty minutes later Stonewall rolled into the parking lot at *Mahsre*. Polanski's Lufthansa flight from Frankfurt should have landed ten minutes earlier. He tipped the attendant and entered the terminal.

Polanski waited in the slow-moving line at customs. The officials immediately recognized Stonewall and, when he indicated the former Special Forces sergeant major, ushered Polanski out of his place and into the private office. Three minutes later the two soldiers of fortune stood on the street.

"You got a lotta pull for only being in-country for a day," the burly Polanski observed. "Where's the nearest beer?"

"Back at the hotel. First we have a little matter to take care of."

That's right, lead me to a whole nest of CIA spies, Imhammad Saghir thought triumphantly while he slid into traffic behind the two Americans. How childishly simple it had been to keep track of the one called Stonewall. His superiors in the Foreign Branch of the *shurtah* would be pleased with his efforts. If only those incompetent fools had not failed him the previous night. The fault was not entirely his, though.

Strict instructions had come from Benghazi that none of the reliable Marxist cells in Cairo were to be contacted in this matter. Absolute secrecy. So, he had been forced to rely upon untrustworthy petty criminals. Achmed Maliq had died for his incompetence. Small consolation, at that, Saghir thought. Now he had to deal with two of the fascist Americans. Stonewall and the one called Hank Polanski. What outlandish names these *farangi* spies had. The two of them together might be hard to handle. Eventual success was his, Saghir knew with assurance.

All it required was to keep the Americans in sight, mark their weaknesses, where they went and when. Then, at the right time . . . Strike!

"Okay, Hank, this is it." Stonewall turned the next corner and pulled his car to the curb half way down the block. Polanski opened the passenger side door and stepped onto the narrow sidewalk. He began to walk away. Behind him, Saghir's Volkswagen entered the street and slowed. Polanski stopped at a shop front, a modern store with plate-glass windows. He used one pane to watch what happened.

The VW slid past Stonewall's parked car, then nosed in to a slot in front. A squat, swarthy man in a short, tunic-like cloak, black trousers and fez, climbed from behind the wheel and walked back to the other vehicle. He peered inside . . .

Directly into the fat muzzle of the McQueen silencer on Stonewall's Sidewinder SMG.

"Don't twitch, creep or I'll send your ass off to Allah."

Swiftly, Polanski raced back to the small sedan and opened the rear door. He wrapped his burly arms around Saghir and bundled him onto the floor, then climbed in after.

"You can sit up and drive now, Cap'n. I got this li'l fucker," Polanski told Stonewall.

An hour later, Imhammad Saghir sprawled rubber-limbed on a couch in Eric Bach's office. A pleasant, re-laxing feeling hummed through his veins and a slack-lipped smile spread over his narrow, sharp-featured Libyan face. At first he had feared death from the needle that had pierced his arm. Now he worried over

51

nothing. The men who had brought him here had been most considerate.

When he had been asked to count backward from one hundred, he had willingly complied. He had done likewise when asked his name, where he lived in Cairo, what he did for a living. A vague alarm seemed to flicker in his mind at that, though he truly felt proud to serve Colonel Qaddafi in the *shurtah*. Why not brag about it a little. The questions grew more pointed, then, asked rapidly and without cease.

"Tell us again," Stonewall snapped, "what was your assignment here?"

"To locate the man called Stonewall and keep him under surveillance until he could be killed."

"What about Madrid?"

"I . . . I don' know. Three men were to wait for Stonewall, kill him. He killed them. Tha's funny."

"Who ordered it?"

"Don' know. I think it wa . . . was Col. Qaddafi personally."

"How did anyone know Stonewall would be in Madrid or here in Cairo?" Eric Bach took over the interrogation.

"Someone gave information to . . . to *shurtah*. Knew Stonewall, Polanski would come. Where, when, what airline. Orders came to kill both men."

"What did Marc Tolliver have to do with it?"

"Who?"

"The American working for Col. Qaddafi," Stonewall provided. He looked intently at the drugged man, willing him to answer.

"Three Americans work for Col. Qaddafi now."

"Where are they, what are they doing?"

"Secret. Not even my superior in Foreign Branch knows."

Erich Bach shot a glance at Stonewall, shook his head.

"He's been through this four times with the same results," Stonewall commented. "I don't think we'll get any more out of him."

"He hasn't anything else to give us," the station chief replied. He crossed to the desk and depressed a tab on the intercom. Two wedge-shaped, hard-eyed young men entered. "Take this garbage out of here and throw it in the Nile," Bach ordered.

Once the men had left, to dispose of Saghir, Eric Bach turned to the two professional soldiers. "I don't like this. It can only mean there is a leak somewhere in Trojan's organization. A traitor who is selling up-to-date information on this operation to Qaddafi."

"That could make things rough going in," Stonewall observed.

"Not necessarily. From what Saghir said, the plan was to stop you outside Libya. With him out of contact, there will be no way of knowing your further movements or even if you are alive. There is every good chance that no one left in the chain knows your itinerary from this point on, maybe never did. In which case, we have a chance."

"We could find ourselves up to our asses in alligators," Polanski provided.

"Can we go in by air?"

"Not possible. The Libyans have grown so paranoid over those jets our navy shot down that they have every known type of warning device installed along the border. Since their buddy Arafat's terrorists wasted Sadat, they expect invasion from Egypt at any time. At least that's what they're telling the world. All the same, the surveillance is tight, too solid to make it in by air. Regardless, you must go on," Eric reminded Stonewall.

"Time is short. They may already have produced functional nuclear weapons. If not Qaddafi will soon have his atomic bombs. When that happens, good-bye to half the cities in the U.S. of A."

Chapter Five

At noon on Monday, an "archeological expedition" lifted off the ground at *Mahsre* International in a creaking old DC-3 to fly the four hundred miles between Cairo and Sidi Barrani. Aboard, along with all the explosives ordered from Eric Bach, rode Stonewall and Polanski. The weight factor had reduced their ammunition and grenade allotment by half. As it was, two rubber boats would have to be used. The roar of the ancient radial engines made conversation impossible. When the lumbering craft touched down, a smiling young Egyptian met Stonewall at the open cargo door.

"I have a truck here to take you to the harbor. Gamel Baudin at your service. *Effendi* Bach sent me."

"We'll give your men a hand with the equipment. Some of it is a bit touchy," Stonewall informed him.

"I understand." Baudin shouted orders in Arabic and four workmen swarmed over the cargo-netted supplies aboard the DC-3. Polanski joined them. Once the off-loading settled into routine, Stonewall took the Egyptian aside.

"What time are we supposed to leave?"

"At two in the morning. That should put you at your debarkation point in the Gulf of Sidra at twenty-two hundred hours tomorrow night."

"That's close to six hundred miles. What are we using?"

"A small coaster of forty-five tons laden has been arranged. It can make thirty-eight knots in an emergency. Cruises at about twenty-five."

"Is it armed?"

Baudin shrugged. "In these waters, in these times, that is a necessity, *effendi.*"

Stonewall allowed himself a wry smile. The whole world seemed to have the same problems. So long as scum like that murder-minded Qaddafi, Arafat and the Assahola Khomeni lived in it and so long as those who opposed them could produce nothing better than spineless pukes like the peanut pusher, it would continue to be plagued by deadly difficulties. But that was why he existed, right? He was there to balance the scale in favor of free men and against the fucking Marxist mob. Right. What was it Patton said about the enemy? *Spill their blood! Shoot them in the belly!* And something about using their living guts to grease the treads of his tanks? Yeah, Georgie had the right idea. No wonder he reached so sudden and untimely an end. Polanski walked up and threw him a two-finger, off-hand salute.

"All aboard, Cap'n. Let's get it on that boat and find some beer."

"Aaah! Beer," Baudin enthused. "Allah forgive me, but I have acquired a great fondness for beer through association with so many Westerners. You will find ten cases aboard the *Malik Bahre,* iced down and waiting for you."

"What about sctoch? Did Eric remember my scotch?"

"Four cases, *effendi* Stonewall, as you ordered."

"Let's get going, then."

Sidi Barrani consisted of a few dirty streets of dwellings for the families of shop workers and farmers, a separate quarter for fishermen and the small business district, built along the only two paved streets in town. Clusters of small, big-eyed children ogled the government truck that rumbled down to quay-side, where the

56

coastal steamer lay along the only large dock. Polanski took one look and shook his head.

"If that's the Sea King, I don't give dittily-squat for our chances of outrunning any patrol boats. If it stays afloat it will be a miracle. A rust-bucket."

Baudin produced a Cheshire grin. "She will do thirty-eight knots, *effendi*. The steam engines have been replaced by modern turbines and the hull has been redesigned below the waterline and fiberglassed for greater speed."

Polanski whistled in appreciation. "Okay, so we have a sleeper here. Where's that beer?"

"You know," Stonewall injected, "I'm beginning to think Swink was right. You're a drunk."

"Fuck Swink. Fuck you, too. Just don't nobody fuck with my beer. A trooper's got to have somethin' to keep him going, right, Cap'n. You officer types have got your fancy scotch and gin, gimme my beer."

Waiting, even with scotch and other emoluments, always elongated the time sense. Every second dragged. Stonewall spent much of it discussing their approach with Polanski.

"We have forty assets. They are all fighting men, at least by their own lights. They know how to ride horses, use swords, spears and rifles. Some have had military training. It will be our job to quickly mold them into fighting like a platoon. We'll each take a section. In the final assault we'll fight as a unit.

"Once the objective has been gained, we split again and take specific targets. You and your men will make a sweep, and destroy any nuclear weapons you find. I'll take my section into the factory, whatever it is. We link up wherever the fighting is heaviest, suppress all resistance and get the hell out of there."

"You mean no more local mucka-mucks keepin' us outta the action so they can play general?"

"Not this time. We lead on this operation. There won't be time to properly train fire teams, so the squads will fight as a unit. We'll employ tactics like those of War Deuce and Korea. Fire and maneuver on a total squad basis. We'll have three Prick-Sixes, one for you, one for the senior squad leader in my section and one with me. Hand and arm signals for everything else."

"How will we be on the numbers?"

"From the time we hit the perimeter until we haul ass can't be more than one hour."

"Tight."

Stonewall swallowed scotch. "If we don't make it by then, the whole Libyan army and air force will be down on us."

"The exfiltration?"

"The Tuaregs will go their way and we go ours, in whatever vehicles are still operational. We strike overland to Egypt."

"Shit."

"No other way, Sergeant. Now, let's get some sack time."

The *Sea King* sailed at two minutes after two the next morning. They negotiated Egyptian waters without incident. The small coaster, running without navigational lights, marked the headlands of *Ra's Amir* before the lookout spotted a Libyan patrol boat.

Immediately the captain ordered the engines throttled back and the *Sea King* ghosted past the lurking gunboat. A tense twenty minutes passed before the low hills of the cape obscured them from the naval vessel and they resumed speed in the waters of the Gulf of Sidra. The change in motion and silent running brought Stonewall and Polanski to the bridge.

"What's happening?" Stonewall inquired through Polanski.

"Libyan patrol boat," came the answer. "We have lost him now."

Ten minutes later, the radar watch announced the presence of a second craft, heading their way at high speed. Once more the captain tried evasive action, swinging further in toward shore to provide a cluttered background for their hunter's electronic search equipment.

"They are slowing," the signalman reported. "But still on the same bearing. About eight minutes away."

Barry Byrd set down his glass of lemon soda and glared at Marc Tolliver. "What do you mean, I'm a Red? A guy's gotta look out for himself, right? How else could I make any money out of that war? The NVA and Charlie were the only side paying for information. I didn't know ideology from owl shit. I was only looking out for number one."

"Well, *I'm* a Red," Pete Guterrez growled. An enormous quantity of Russian vodka had turned his eyes into burning red dots. "Have been since I was a kid. Let the fuckin' Anglos or someone steal your country and oppress you for more'n a hundred years and see if you don't take help wherever you can get it. I remember one time in Saigon, I was on R and R, I met these three grunts. Turns out they're *compadres* to some of my nieces and nephews. We'd all been in the Brown Beret, Chicano thing through our teens. There wasn't a project the Communist Party gave us we hadn't been a part of. From taking that Highway Patrol building away from the pigs down in San Diego and turnin' it into a People's Park, to the demonstrations in Los Angeles and with Chavez's union, boy, we were there."

"How is it none of that showed up on your security clearances?" Tolliver inquired.

"Lucky I guess. I never got busted, never had anyone

identify me as a member of the movement. But my grandmother spoon fed me on hating the *gringos*. When I got older my teachers gave me more and I met kids in the street gangs. Jesus, I was a skinny little thing, scared of my own shadow. Next thing you know I was readin' the *Daily Worker* and shoutin' 'Power to the People!' I helped blow a pig away back in sixty-five. Next year I joined the army."

"You're a real credit to your country, Guterrez," Barry dryly commented.

"Fuckin'-A I am. Anyway, my *compadres* an' me got so fuckin' *borracho*. I couldn't focus my eyes for two days. Got to singin' Civil Rights songs. Threw some slopes outta this bar an' the MP pigs came. They thumped our heads and hauled our buns off to the stockade. First and last time I ever had any bad shit on me in the army. You were supposed to be Mr. Clean, too, Major. Tell us, what's the real shit behind that club rip-off scam?"

Marc Tolliver started to make a reply when the door opened. Standing in the dimly lighted underground corridor was Captain Boris Zmeyá. The KGB agent smiled broadly and entered the recreation room, where the three Americans sat drinking. Two stainless steel molars glinted in the otherwise snowy perfection of his small, reptilian teeth. His big, peasant hands looked awkward hanging at his sides.

"Later, Pete." Tolliver turned his attention to the Soviet agent. "Good evening, Captain. Rather, I should say, good morning. We're enjoying our day off with a little of your vodka. Join us?"

"No. Or, rather, yes. This is a time for celebration. The project is drawing closer to success." Zmeyá poured a glass of *Stolichnaya* and his pale brown eyes glowed. Although past his fortieth birthday, not a strand of gray showed in his curly, ochre hair. "Your services have been invaluable, Tolliver. I must say you deserve the rank of Colonel given to you by Muammar Qaddafi. In the Libyan forces, of course." He raised the small crystal flute in salute. *"Zah vah-sheh zdahrohv'yeh!"*

"To your good health, too, Captain," Tolliver replied in Russian. They drank and Zmeyá poured refills for all.

"Tell me, now that the production of the atomic weapons nears completion, how shall they be employed?"

Tolliver looked thoughtful a moment. "I'm not certain I can divulge that right now."

"Come now. We are men of the world, no? You must be aware that the Soviet government is not the least concerned if some nation, say of the Third World, conducts a nuclear attack on the United States. Our only insistence is that it in no way be possible to trace the origin of that assault back to the Soviet Union. To be sure of that, precise information is needed on the method of employment."

Smokey whorls developed in Marc Tolliver's opaque eyes. "Surely the Soviet Union is in a position to be most, ah, generous to anyone providing them such valuable information?"

"How much is it worth, in other words?"

"You are a perceptive man, Boris."

"Fifty thousand U.S. dollars, for each of you naturally, in a Swiss bank account."

"Done," Tolliver agreed for them all. "When the production ends, there will be twelve bombs. They will be transported on ships of foreign registry, Panamanian primarily, and enter the target areas on board several of them.

"Those are the ones for the St. Lawrence Seaway, Boston, New York and Washington, D.C. Also New

Orleans and Houston, Texas. Those slated for Chicago, and Colorado Springs will be taken across the border with Mexico. Asiatic ships will bring the bombs into Seattle, San Francisco, Los Angeles and San Diego."

"Do you anticipate it will be really be that easy?"

"Of course. Most will be dropped overboard for underwater blasts. Very dirty, radiation wise, with little blast and fire damage. For those brought in by land it's a simple matter. There are miles of border that aren't carefully policed. Not enough men or equipment. If the fools had done away with it long ago and made one country, it would be much harder."

"Yes. Fortunately, your previous president so alienated the government and people of Mexico, that it is easy for us to use them as tools. At least for the present."

"What about the future?" Barry Byrd inquired. "The Hollywood Cowboy has become a thorn in your sides, right? And the Mexes seem to like him, too."

"Only a temporary inconvenience. We will either control him, as we have managed to do in the past with other, less, ah, intractable presidents, or he will be eliminated. But it is not our place to discuss such high level policy. What is to happen once the bombs are in place?"

"Six of them will go off within twenty-four hours and then Col. Qaddafi issues his ultimatum. The United States will capitulate or other bombs will be set off, one a day until surrender."

Insanity! Boris Zmeyá thought in a flash. No one is more zealous than a convert and these Americans were certainly proving the old axiom. Surely they realized such a rash action would mean war. When that happened, as predicted at Moscow Center, the Soviet Union would easily step in and take over both countries. Oh, well, it accomplished his government's goal either way. His only responsibility was to see that the

Soviet technicians left safely or died here, unidentified. He forced a smile.

"A great plan, if you can carry it off. It should place you quite high in Col. Qaddafi's favor. When are the first bombs to be shipped?"

"Within a week."

"Please illuminate navigation lights and heave to." The Arabic words crackled across the water separating the patrol boat from the *Malik Bahre*. The captain glanced helplessly at Stonewall and Polanski; shrugged and complied.

"What can we do?" he plaintively asked his passengers.

"You've got a forty millimeter and two fifty machineguns on this tub. Have their crews ready and standing by. Then stall the Libyans for as long as you can. Polanski, go below," Stonewall continued, immediately grasping the situation. "Bring me one of the RDX satchel charges and a big-ass magnet if you can find one in the engine room. I want a pencil detonator with a max setting of three minutes."

"Right, Cap'n. Want me to do the dirty work?"

"Naw, this one's all mine."

"Have your papers ready and stand by to receive boarders." The order rattled from the hand-held bullhorn on the flying bridge of the cruiser.

"Tell 'em something to stall, Captain," Stonewall snapped.

"Hello the patrol boat. This is Captain Harmudz. We have sickness aboard."

"Do you wish a doctor? What is your sickness?"

"Tell him the fuckin' plague, for Christsake," Stonewall hissed. "Anything. We need time."

"What for, *effendi* Stonewall?"

"In a few seconds I'm leaving your ship. When I've

been gone two minutes, I want you to start letting her drift off to port a little. Don't worry, I can catch up. I want lots of room between us and that gunboat out there."

"Why? They have spotlights. We can not get the guns in action without having them fire on us."

"I'm gonna blow that tub out of the fucking water. Or I hope so. By the time I get back on board, have the crews run to their guns. When she blows, then we open fire."

"By Allah! Are you mad? Or . . ." A grim smile creased the captain's seamed face. "It might work at that. You will have our cooperation, *effendi.*"

"I'd better, or it's all our asses."

"Here you are, Cap'n," Polanski announced cheerfully.

"All right. Down on deck, on the side away from the Libyans. Captain, lower the port gangway."

Stonewall reached the main deck and began removing his clothing. A small engine coughed to life and cable began to pay out, lowering the boarding stair. Polanski worked with the explosive package, positioning the magnet and inserting the timepencil through the diaphragm in the middle of the RDX.

"What is that noise?" Do not attempt to abandon ship!" the Libyan commander yelled.

"Our starboard gangway is broken. We are lowering the port one to receive your boarding party."

"Very well, proceed."

A fleeting minute later, Stonewall ran down the inclined steps and slid into the water.

Strong, powerful strokes took the white-haired soldier of fortune far wide of the prow of the stopped coaster. In darkness he pulled toward the distant patrol craft. Using the silent, sideways style called the Special Forces crawl, he rapidly drew near. A slight chop kept him invisible to the sailors aboard the Libyan ship. The chill of the Mediterranean water seeped into his bare flesh and he forced his mind to ignore it, counting strokes and pausing every few seconds to check his bearing. With a final heave he skimmed past under the bow and rounded the iron vessel's forepeak.

Stonewall tread water while his fingers sought a flat, barnacle-free space large enough to receive the magnet. The small shell creatures flayed at his finger pads, blood streaming away into the water, until at last he located a patch of metal, slimy with neglect, though free of barnacles. Gently, Stonewall eased the heavy explosive package into place, poised to let it attach to the hull. A loud splash from the opposite side caused him to freeze. His head went below the waves.

Only a dinghy being lowered to accommodate the boarding party, Stonewall realized when he saw the bubble trail of a small outboard motor swirling under the keel. He forced his way to the surface and resumed his task.

Stonewall kept his fingers widespread over the canvas covering the magnet to prevent a loud sound transmitting through the bulkhead and alerting the crew when he made the attachment. An inch more now. Easy, he cautioned himself. Weight dragged at his arms, urging him to hurry. The satchel charge tilted toward the ship's side. Cautiously he slid the fingers of his left hand free and eased down the magnet.

Now the right.

Stonewall gusted out a sigh when the soft thud that came ended his ordeal. He removed the safety pin from the barrel of the time pencil and twisted the gnurled knob to the three minute position, then began his swim back to the *Sea King*.

Chapter Six

"Captain, stop your boat from drifting!" A burst of 20mm fire across the bow of the *Sea King* emphasized the Libyan officer's command. Stonewall struck out in a hard, fast racing crawl.

Another salvo of whirring 20mm slugs hummed over his head. Stonewall realized he had cut too far into the lighted area between boats. He veered right.

Twenty powerful strokes brought him within sight of the looming coastal steamer. Ten more put him in line with the bow. Thirty got him around to the unlighted port side. The boarding party's dinghy had arrived. One Libyan sailor stood on the small, square platform to guard the craft. Stonewall submerged and swam forward.

Only the smallest ripple of disturbed water betrayed the soldier of fortune's arrival at the gangway. He rose out of the sea and grabbed the unsuspecting Libyan from behind, one powerful arm around the man's neck, his knee driving into the small of the sailor's back. Stonewall's free hand held a Sykes-Fairbaine commando knife, which he slid into the space behind his victim's left collarbone.

Steel grated on flesh and muscle, biting deeply into a lung. Stonewall slashed it back and forth, severing the subclavian artery. He withdrew the bloodied blade and drove it into the dying Libyan's kidney, then eased the body over the side. Quietly, on bare feet, he ran up the ladder toward the main deck.

"Now!" Stonewall shouted as his mental stopwatch

ticked off the vital three minutes of the time pencil. Polanski stepped onto the deck and cut down two Libyans with his M-14.

Suddenly the sun rose in the north.

Bright orange light filled the horizon, silhouetting the doomed patrol boat for a brief second before the blast and concussion traveled across the heaving water to the coaster. Immediately figures scurried along the deck, uncovering the hidden guns, inserting breech blocks and slapping ammunition into open receivers.

The twenty millimeter belched first, then the forty. Lines of green tracers, from the Soviet made arms and ammunition, streaked toward the Libyan vessel. For a moment, return fire brightened the night. Then, with a groan like a dying whale, the gunboat rolled onto its starboard side and sank, barnical-encrusted keel disappearing last into a whirlpool of white foam.

A Libyan officer ran toward Stonewall, his mouth open in a scream of rage, a U.S. Government Model .45 in one hand. The muzzle started to swing toward Stonewall's middle. Armed with only a knife, the soldier for hire looked at Death and recognized his old companion coming for the final reaping.

From the corner of his eye, Stonewall saw a metallic blur streaking through the air toward him. Reflexively he reached out and caught the Sidewinder. He racked back the cocking knob and his finger closed on the trigger. A short, three-round burst slammed its familiar triangular pattern into the Libyan's chest. A look of utter disbelief crossed the officer's face. He had seen that the American was unarmed. An easy kill. Why, then, was it him who was dying?

He had little time to contemplate one of life's most bitter questions. Stonewall sent a single .45 slug crashing into the Libyan's face, exploding shards of bone and teeth into the brain. The naval ensigns' legs continued to churn forward while his upper body whipped rearward. He went over backward, dead before his skull cracked on the metal deck plates.

Quickly the sounds of battle ended.

"Duck, Cap'n!" Polanski shouted and, when Stonewall went to one knee, shot a Libyan sailor armed with a Matt-49 French submachine gun who had appeared from around the pilot house and taken aim at Stonewall's back.

"Get under way, Captain," Stonewall called to the bridge. "We can dump bodies after we're moving."

"*Iwah, effendi,*" the coaster's commander responded cheerfully. "Iss one hell of a fight, no?" he continued in broken English.

Half an hour later, running now at full speed, the *Sea King* slid past Esso's offshore tanker loading terminal at Marsa el Brega. No huge oil transports were moored to the buoys. Since the earlier U.S. embargo of Libyan oil, most European nations had grudgingly and reluctantly followed suit. With the other Arab League nations suffering from a glut of their own crude, Qaddafi's Marxist regime had no one to buy from them. Served the stupid fucker right, Stonewall thought. Qaddafi had apparently not been smart enough to realize there existed a marked difference between the pussy who sat in the rose garden and let fifty-one Americans languish in the hands of rag-head fanatics in Iran and the ballsey Irishman who occupied the Oval Office now.

Qaddafi had to be as crazy as his look-alike, Jim Jones, Stonewall reflected. First he tries to intimidate the U.S. Navy, and gets two of his jets trashed for his efforts. Then he sends assassins after top American officials, only to have them turn yellow and slink off in Mexico or Canada somewhere to hide. Now he wants to start a nuclear war, so hopelessly one sided that he'll be lucky if it doesn't end with Libya being a large radio active sheet of glass. Might be a good idea at that. The thin wail of a distant siren drew Stonewall's attention to the heaving breast of the Gulf of Sidra.

Another Libyan patrol boat struggled vainly to close with the pulsing *Sea King*. Even while he watched, Stonewall could easily discern that the contest would have but one result. Outclassed by the unsuspected power plant of the *Sea King*, the naval craft had no hope of coming into firing range, let alone overhauling the coaster. He continued to observe for another fifteen minutes until the Libyan gunboat disappeared over the horizon.

"Another half hour, *effendi* Stonewall," the captain spoke from behind him. "I am worried about a storm coming in off the Mediterranean. We have it on radar. There is a chance it will reach here about the time we let you off between Sirte and An Nawfaliyah."

"You are filled with good news and cheerful predictions."

The captain shrugged. "The sea is a harsh mistress," he replied philosophically.

Stonewall grabbed at the rail in front of him when a large wave nearly threw him off his feet. He grinned mischievously. "But she sure knows how to hump."

"Aah! You *do* understand. You would have made a great sailor, *effendi* Stonewall."

"Thank you, Captain." The solider for hire left the flying bridge to find Polanski. They would spend the next fifteen minutes organizing their gear for debarcation.

"Careful with that stuff, you son of a he-camel," Polanski growled in Arabic at a crewman. "You could blow us right out of the water."

Silently the *Sea King* drifted off the shore of Libya,

near the southern-most indentation of the Gulf of Sidra. Two large rubber rafts, each equipped with silent running electric outboard motors, had been inflated and lowered to the plunging surface of the sea. The Egyptian sailors labored to off-load explosives and ammunition in a rising wind that brought with it choppy, spume-flecked rollers that threatened to become churning masses of deadly green water. At last the task ended. Stonewall and Polanski slipped over the side to take charge of their unstable craft. The captain wished them luck and signaled the engine room to get under way.

Spray whipped over the blunt bow of the lead boat and wet Stonewall to the skin. At least the coming storm approached from behind them. The pressure of wind and wave would speed the trip ashore and provide some additional cover. Already the stars disappeared behind an advancing line of black clouds. The moon had disappeared before they left the protective side of the *Sea King*.

They rode in literally under the guns of the Libyan navy and security forces. Radar, spotlights and sophisticated detection devices protected the shore. If the *Sea King's* captain had worked his navigation problems correctly, though, they should run onto the beach at a point lightly guarded by a company of poorly trained, inexperienced troops. For a moment, Stonewall felt grateful for the squall that swept in from the north.

Suddenly the leading edge of the rain caught up and poured over him. Stonewall lost track of Polanski's boat, running to his left and half a length behind. A gray curtain of hissing wetness blinded him and he tried to locate the beach and maintain his orientation.

Unremitting, the deluge continued. Water accumulated in the bottom of the rubber craft, which heaved on the angry waves and tried to turn sideways. Stonewall fought it. A huge following sea lifted the wallowing craft and smashed it down in the next trough. Stonewall's sense of direction reeled and he thought he heard a muffled shout from where Polanski should be. Of all times for a distraction, a troubling thought rose. Would their Tuareg guide be there with the jeep and trailer? He battered the disturbing element from his mind and tried to concentrate on keeping his back to the wind. There, that way, to the south was where he wanted to go.

How did I get on this roller coaster? The sensation increased with the violence of the storm. Limited to a few feet of gray nothingness, Stonewall's vision gave him no help. He thought he spun around, a complete three-sixty, at one point, then the wind slammed at him from the port, stern quarter and the foundering raft began to move sideways. The gunwales nearly awash, Stonewall had to release the steering arm of the electric motor with one hand to bail with a gallon can, provided by the skipper of the *Sea King*. He wondered where Polanski had gotten to.

Hank Polanski fought his own grim battle with the sea. The moment he lost sight of Stonewall he lost all sense of direction. Wind and wave pushed him first one way, then the other. He stubbornly held onto the tiller, the tiny outboard labored wide open. A following crest lifted the raft high above the water and the small prop spun wildly in the air, then slammed into the green spume that ran slickly over the green sheet. Polanski gnawed at the inner surface of his lower lip and tried to find the darker silhouette of land in the swirling miasma of the squall.

Stonewall struggled hopelessly against the filling raft. Weighted by over six hundred pounds of material, the eight man craft tried to drag him to the bottom of the Gulf. One more big one, he estimated, only one and he would be swamped.

71

Damn the sea for trying to rob him of a chance to kill more commies. Damn it! He couldn't, he wouldn't let it defeat him.

Chapter Seven

With a final, vicious lash of stinging drops, the squall swirled past, racing inland. Wind-whipped waves continued to toss the rubber boats around like chaff on a pond. Gradually, Stonewall could make out a dark, low lying mass off to his right. He fought to resist the forces of the storm and align himself with the distant shore. There appeared to be a long, undulating upslope between his position and the beach. Sluggishly, his fragile craft began to obey the force directing it. Its stubborn behavior brought Stonewall back to his most immediate problem.

Although running with the wind, sheets of water slopped over the low-riding gunwales. Stonewall began to bail, throwing out a gallon of water at a time. He seemed to make little headway. The sound of tempest-born breakers came clearly over the howl of the gale before he perceived a noticable reduction in the water on board and the corresponding rising of the raft. He put aside the can and concentrated on steering.

Another ten, hard-fought minutes brought the bobbing yellow raft to the top of the seething incline. Quickly Stonewall yanked the tiller to one side, running parallel to the thundering breakers that could swamp him. He gauged the curl like a surfer and timed his swing toward the beach to ride out the best part of the wave. Precariously he held to the small rope railing with one hand, tensed to act on an instant's impulse.

Hit it!

A long, pealing curve shot the raft forward. It spun

and gyrated in mad abandon that abruptly ended with a jarring crunch when the blunt prow dug into shelving sand. Stonewall slithered over the side, felt his feet make firm contact with the bottom and threw his shoulders into the effort of dragging the obstinate burden up above the waterline. With a final powerful heave he managed the task, though the exertion sent him sprawling on the damp sand. Stonewall looked up to see a pair of boots, a foot from his face.

"What took you so long, Cap'n?" Polanski asked, extending a hand to help Stonewall rise.

"I wouldn't believe that from anyone but you," the rangy soldier for hire responded while he came to his feet. A dozen feet away, a Libyan soldier lay in the grotesque sprawl of death. His throat had been slit. "We'd better drag that away along with my raft."

"Right, Cap'n. I found a nice cluster of rocks a little ways from here." He walked to the corpse, hefted it and carried it to the rubber boat. Then Polanski returned to brush out any signs of the brief struggle. "Be better if we carry that. Won't have to come back."

"Any sign of our guide?"

"Naw. Only a hell of a lot of Libyan troops."

"They're here to repell, 'invasion by hordes of CIA terrorists and assassins,' as Qaddafi put it."

"My, my, I failed to be properly impressed."

"Lift, we can talk later."

With a grunt, the Hulk lifted one side of the raft while Stonewall took the other. They reached the jumble of aged, decaying boulders in two minutes and began assembling the supplies.

"Did you give any thought to just how in hell we're supposed to get this stuff off the beach?"

"You've got a back, don't you?"

"Jesus, Cap'n. We go stompin' around loaded down with all that crap it'll make more noise than elephants screwin'. There's gotta be a better way."

Stonewall gathered the straps of several satchel charges and slid them over his left shoulder and hung the Sidewinder by its sling from the opposite one. He grabbed an ammunition can in each hand. "When you think of one, let me know."

"Aaawh, shit, Cap'n." Polanski loaded up and followed behind, protest stilled by the close presence of Libyan soldiers. He lifted his feet carefully, avoiding any excessive noise.

Bent low, both men worked their way to the top of a ridge of rolling sand dunes. As one, they went to their bellies and crawled to the crest. Beyond their vantage point lay a low belt of prickly salt bush and thorn. On the other side of that, according to the map Stonewall had studied, should be the roadway. There was no sign of Libyan outposts or patrols.

"We'll take the gear to the far side of that row of brush and go back for another load."

"That's askin' for it, Cap'n. No tellin' when the Libyans will get wise to us."

"You see any sign of troops around here?"

"No," the big ex-sergeant had to admit.

"Maybe that sentry you wasted was a roving patrol. This is supposed to be the least guarded part of the coast."

"I won't make book on it, though right now I'll lay ten to one we don't get away with this."

"I'll take a hundred dollars worth of that."

"Balls."

Half way back with the second load, Stonewall halted Polanski with a sudden hand signal. In the distance could be heard the whine of an approaching jeep engine.

"Let's get out of sight in those bushes."

Polanski darted forward. "Don't have to ask me twice."

Screened by the thick scrub, Stonewall and Polanski waited for the oncoming vehicle. Each held his weapon at the ready. Dim headlights came into view. The slanted rays yellowed the sand over which the soldiers of fortune had scurried with their burdens. Stonewall raised his Sidewinder.

The jeep halted.

Soft, indistinct words floated across the hundred feet distance. The driver engaged the gear, cramped his wheels and backed at a right angle to their path. He changed the shift lever, rotated the tires in the opposite direction and accelerated.

"Close," Polanski exhaled.

"Enough," Stonewall agreed. Quickly they resumed their relay.

For the third trip, Polanski tucked a case of AK-47's under each massive arm and Stonewall gathered the remaining ammo cans. On an undefined hunch the white haired soldier for hire broke his assegai out of the A-frame pack and attached its leather sheath to his belt. Their exertions had first dried their salt-water encrusted clothes, then saturated them in sweat. Stonewall itched in each armpit and his feet felt pressure cooked. Two more loads, he estimated with a glance at the remaining supplies. So far they had been lucky, he knew. If it would only hold.

Back at the growing mound of weapons and explosives, a Libyan soldier spraddle-legged over the accumulation. A stupefied look blanked his face and he held his assault rifle in an awkward approximation of port arms. His height over the obstructing brush warned Stonewall in time to prevent scratching limbs and crackling twigs from giving away their presence. Polanski halted immediately behind him.

Stonewall set down his burden and silently drew his assegai. Crouched low, hands and feet moving with all

76

the coordinated skill of his Cherokee ancestors, Stonewall eased his way forward. The Libyan, a member of a paramilitary police security unit, turned away, set down his rifle and unslung a handheld radio from his left shoulder. Before he opened his mouth to speak the words that would spell destruction for the infiltrating soldiers for hire, Stonewall leaped from the brush.

A heavy brass ball formed the pommel of the assegai. Stonewall smashed it into the back of the Libyan's skull, quickly reversed his grip and drove the sharp, leaf-bladed weapon to the hilt in the unfortunate soldier's back. The tip protruded from the center of his chest in a shower of blood. Stonewall eased him to the ground.

"Shit. More trouble. Let's move fast."

In five minutes they came back with a fourth load. Polanski looked like he could drink a medium-sized brewery dry. "Damn glad there's nothin' left but our packs and another case of AK's," he panted.

"Yeah," Stonewall answered dryly. "That and finding our guide."

The final trip went without incident.

Now came the hard part.

Stonewall and Polanski parted and walked along the road in opposite directions. Heavy cloud cover still obscured the moon, a break for them. A little rough for spotting possible ambushes, though. Stonewall got within thirty feet of a parked jeep before he recognized its darker shape against the groundline. It fit the description of the one they were looking for, complete with empty trailer. One small, nagging problem remained. No sight of the guide.

"Claw the air, pilgrim," a voice, in fair imitation of Duke Wayne, called softly from behind Stonewall.

"What the h . . ."

"I am Bashir Fawzi, your guide. You are Stonewall, I presume?"

"You tryin' to get your ass blown away?" Stonewall snapped, angry more at being taken by surprise than at the guide's decision to not wait in plain sight by the jeep.

"Touchy. I like that in a man." A short, cockily strutting Tuareg stepped from the brush, an old M-2 U.S. Carbine held loosely in both hands.

"What's with the John Wayne bit?"

Fawzi's eyes lit, even in the darkness, with zeal. "John Wayne was the greatest American ever born. Maybe the greatest man ever. I have seen him at the cinema many times. I want to live like he did."

An amused smile creased Stonewall's leathery, lined cheeks. "A guy could do worse for an idol, I suppose. The supplies are down the road a bit. We'd better get back."

Fawzi climbed behind the wheel and started the engine. "At your service, *effendi* Stonewall."

Sand spurted from under the jeep's wheels and the engine roared in protest while the empty trailer rattled and banged loudly enough to arouse a deaf-mute. Fawzi seemed unconcerned over any potential danger. They reached the stack of goods in less than a minute and Fawzi began to load while Stonewall went in search of Polanski.

He found him three hundred yards down the beach, headed back. "What the fuck's that guy got, a tank?"

"No. He thinks he's Duke Wayne and Evil Kanevil all rolled into one. We'd better load up and get out of here before half the Libyan army falls on us."

The loading went quickly. When only two items remained, Polanski suddenly stiffened. He cocked his ear to one side. One huge, hairy paw flew to his left side and closed around the handle of a vintage USMC bolo-machette. He swiftly whirled to his right, drawing the heavy, round-tipped weapon with blurring speed. The thick, wedge-shaped blade glimmered dully in the dim light for a moment before it made a meaty smacking sound.

A Lybian soldier's head fell into the sand and rolled three feet from his slack body, which crumpled onto the ground, twin columns of blood geysering high into the night sky. Polanski wiped clean his deadly tool on the tan uniform jacket of his victim and returned the bolo-machette to its scabbard.

"Sneaky bastard," the retired sergeant major grumbled. "Wanted to get right on top of us before he blew us to doll rags."

"How did you do that? I mean, so fast."

"You like that? Some day I'll teach you how."

"First we have to evade about a thousand Libyan security troops," Stonewall reminded them.

"Oh, that," Fawzi dismissed lightly. "There is only a twenty man patrol along this stretch of coast at night. I disposed of two of them on the way in. With those you have eliminated it makes our risk very slim." He fired up the jeep and three heads snapped back when he popped the clutch.

"You might as well get some sleep," Fawzi advised. "The drive to Sharif Mammaudz's encampment will take two days."

"Why is that?"

"It is six hundred of your miles, most of it in the desert, on dirt roads."

"Lovely," Polanski growled. "Just fucking lovely."

Chapter Eight

Two days of sun, dryness and desolation left Stonewall and Polanski hungering for the sight of another human being, any form of building and all the water they could consume, roll in and gaze upon. The first indication that the journey had come to an end was a stand of tall, thick-trunked date palms. Over a dust-hazed rise the occupants of the jeep discovered the low, black tents of the Tuareg band led by Sharif Achmed Mammaudz. Within five minutes they reached the oasis.

"I never thought *water'd* look so damned good," Polanski summed up when he climbed from the sturdy quarter-ton vehicle.

A crowd quickly gathered. Fierce-eyed tribesmen, their features hidden inside the hoods of their burnooses, ringed the jeep. Behind them clustered the women and big-eyed children. Dust, which had traveled with them in an elongated plume, boiled over the scene. When it dissipated the Tuaregs in front of the vehicle had drawn to either side, leaving a corridor. At the far end of the opening stood an impressive figure.

He wore baggy felt trousers and a kaftan robe, both of a rich blue color that denoted Tuareg nobility, and instead of the usual burnoose, his head was covered by the typically Arabic *kafeyah* and *agal*. The cloth headdress was of the same azure color as his clothing, the twin cords braided of gold and white. Pointed-toe boots of bright red leather completed the outfit. In his right hand he carried a camel's tail riding crop. His left closed around the silver inlaid scabbard of a long sword. Slowly, with a grand, stately majesty, he approached the arrivals.

"Your Excellency, Sharif Achmed Mammaudz, may I present Mr. J. C. Stonewall of the United States," Bashir Fawzi began in the Tuareg dialect, then switched to English. "Mr. Stonewall it is my privilege to present you to his Excellency, *Hadj* Achmed Mammaudz, Sharif of the al Hamdillah Tuaregs."

Stonewall extended his hand. "A pleasure to meet you, sir."

The Sharif stared at Stonewall's arm, unfamiliar with the Western gesture, until Fawzi whispered to the American. "You are supposed to bow."

"Oh." Stonewall inclined his head and slightly tilted his shoulders. That was as far as he would ever bow to another man.

"Welcome to the Oasis of el Harum, Mr. Stonewall," the Sharif greeted him in Tuareg. "This is your associate, I presume?"

"Yes, sir. Sergeant-Major Hank Polanski."

"*Asalamu alaicum, ya Sharif,*" Polanski responded, bobbing his head in imitation of Stonewall's gesture.

Mammaudz's face brightened. "*Wialaicum is-salam.* You speak our language well for a foreigner," he went on.

"Thank you, sir."

A strikingly attractive young woman came forward from among the onlookers. Unlike the other women, she did not wear the traditional Tuareg costume. Tight-fitting trousers, cut in the Spanish style, encased well-formed legs and an equally snug bolero jacket stretched to cover pert, full breasts that could not be de-emphasized by a frilly-fronted white blouse. Like the Sharif, the dominant color of her clothing was blue. Her head was bare, revealing long, lustrous black hair and a leather thong at her throat restrained a flat-crown Cordovan sombrero that rested lightly on her cascade of raven locks. She stopped beside the Sharif and looked inquiringly into his face.

A man of medium height, which made him tall for a Tuareg, the Sharif seemed embarrassed by her presence. "Gentlemen, my daughter, Najid bint Mammaudz. You must forgive her brazen appearance. She is—how do you put it?—a somewhat liberated woman."

"A scandal is how you generally describe me, father." She extended a hand toward Stonewall. "How do you do? I am most happy to have you here." She had a flawless command of English.

Stonewall shook her hand, her warm, graceful fingers encased in his hard fist. "A pleasure. What should I call you?"

"Najid is good enough. And you? What do the initials stand for?"

"Nothing. Just Jay-Cee. Call me Stonewall, Najid."

Polanski could not miss the heightened interest of his boss when Stonewall looked closely at the oval face, creamy complexion and strong, patrician nose of the young woman, whose hand he had not yet released. "I hate to interrupt this pleasant *tête-à-tête*, but we came here to do a job, remember?" he growled.

"Right." Stonewall dropped Najid's hand. "Is Philmore Nichols here?" he asked the Sharif.

"No. Your Mr. Nichols has been in contact but remains in Tripoli for the moment. He will join us later."

"What about the troops?"

Sharif Mammaudz beamed with pride. His eyes, widely set from a large, hawk-billed nose, danced with highlights. "Volunteers from other tribes have been arriving over the past week. You have the promised complement of forty men, with a few to spare."

"That's good. We will start training tomorrow morning," the soldier of fortune informed his host.

Achmed Mammaudz looked surprised. "We have planned a feast in your honor. That will take all of tomorrow. We are most happy and wish to celebrate this opportunity to strike a blow against the communists who have taken over the country and seek to destroy our way of life."

"I've never been one to turn down a chance to party, but time is short. We will start at dawn the day after tomorrow, then."

"Ah! Excellent," the Sharif enthused.

Ten goats, from the numerous flocks that belonged to the tribe, had been roasted for the feast. A large table, made of planks and sawhorses, had been set up in the shade of date palms beside the pool of water that gave life to the oasis. It swayed under the weight of huge cheeses, baskets of dates, onions, peppers and other condiments. From early morning the air had been redolent with the odors of cooking. Before the day's festivities began, Stonewall and Polanski spent the time talking with small groups of the Tuareg volunteers.

"Are any of you familiar with the Soviet assault rifle?" Stonewall inquired of each group through Polanski's translations.

"The Kalashnikov?" one young man remarked. "Yes. I have fired it often. I was, for two years, in the Libyan army," he ended proudly.

"Good. For now you are temporary squad leader over these eight men. If you work out, you'll keep that post for the attack. You will all be armed with AK-47's. You will also have hand grenades, both fragmentation and white phosphorous."

With another gathering, he added to the usual questions, "Have any of you fired a Russian rocket gun?"

"The RPG-24?" asked a stout, mustacheod Tuareg in his mid-thirties.

"That's the one."

"We took some from a patrol that had been sent to force my tribe into a city to live. I learned how to load and fire it. A powerful weapon."

83

"Could you hit anything?"

"Oh, yes."

"You'll do. You'll be with me and two others in the headquarters section. Could you teach some of the others to use them?"

"Certainly. But we have none."

"We'll get them . . . the same way you got yours."

A round of eager smiles accompanied the translation of Stonewall's words. By noon the food was ready. Everyone gathered under the trees.

Wild music skirled an accompaniment to the banquet. Stonewall sat in the place of honor, to the Sharif's right, with Polanski on the older man's left. Najid sat beside the white-haired soldier for hire. Ornate carpets in bold designs had been spread on the sand, heaped with fat pillows for the diners' comfort. Stonewall reclined against a pile of the latter, eating *cous-cous* with a two finger scooping action in imitation of his host. Najid spoke only a few banal pleasantries before she started to ply Stonewall with questions about America.

"I broke with all tradition, you see," she said by way of explanation. "I was educated in England. I met many Americans there, but never had the opportunity to travel in your country. Tell me, is it true that all American women have big . . " she held both cupped hands under her own nicely developed breasts. "Ah, bosoms?"

Stonewall grinned and nodded. "And nice round bottoms, too. But the truth is there aren't many of them who could compare well with you. You're really a lovely young woman, you know."

Deep dimples, that added a little-girl charm to Najid's exquisite features, formed at the corners of her mouth and she blushed slightly. "Why, thank you, Stonewall. I'm not accustomed to compliments."

"Now that I don't believe."

"I mean here, among my own people. Our women are considered more like property. Like goats and camels."

"I'm sure that might apply to some. On the other hand, you . . ." The looming shadow of a young, bow-legged Tuareg interrupted Stonewall's flattery. He looked up to see an anger-flushed face thrust toward him, the eyes glittering obsidian daggers.

"I am Ali Hammad al Taliq. Your presence here offends Allah, the al Hamdillah Tuaregs and me. You claim to be a warrior, but I see you to be soft and decadent. I demand that you prove yourself in a trial of personal combat."

Stonewall looked at Najid. "What the hell is he talking about?"

"Ali Hammad has challenged you to a contest of arms. It is a traditional Tuareg test of a man's skills and courage, to prove his worth as a warrior."

"Do I have to go through with this?"

From the other side of the Sharif, who looked on in cold disapproval, Polanski belched loudly. "You'd better take him up on it, Cap'n. These little fellers are tough as dinosaur turds. They're gonna want to see what we're made of sooner or later, before they'll follow us into action."

The Sharif spoke briefly and Polanski translated. "He says that to refuse such a challenge is an automatic brand as a coward. He regrets you have been put to it in this manner, by a low-born half-breed, but all the same, it's shit or get off the pot."

Stonewall studied his accuser. The young man's skin seemed lighter than most Tuaregs, his features more regular and smooth, almost Anglo in cut. A half-breed? Yes, he could be. With a shrug Stonewall rose to his feet.

"What is it I am supposed to do?"

85

"There are three parts to the contest," the Sharif explained through Polanski. "First to prove horsemanship, second prowess with arms and finally to show strength and agility."

"Horses I understand. How do we go about the other two?"

"Traditional Tuareg weapons will be used, the lance and sword. The last part is a grappling match. He probably means wrestling, Cap'n," Polanski added.

"How far is this thing to be carried?"

Polanski asked and the Sharif answered. "Only until blood has been drawn. No one is to die."

"That's a comfort," Stonewall observed acidly. "All right, let's get on with it."

A great cheer rose from the assembled tribesmen. The women jabbered excitedly and children raced each other to reach advantageous spots along the wide games ground. Preparations began at once.

Four men strapped a straw-packed mattress to a tall, upright post, while two others attached a long chain to its crossarm. Affixed to the other end of the links was a palmwood ball, studded with date thorns. When the workmen stood clear, a teenage boy, perched on a small pedestal, heaved on the horizontal bar and spun it around. Satisfied, he called for a helmeted goat-hide ball, stuffed with straw, which he fastened to the top of the post to form the "head." Meanwhile other efforts were being made.

Six Tuaregs drove pointed stakes into the ground, ten paces apart. When they finished, small red flags were tied to each. A dozen others, laughing and shouting, pulled a stone-weighted, spike-tooth wooden harrow over the ground, smoothing and leveling it. Stonewall went to the tent he had been given for living quarters to make ready.

"Are you gonna use that African toothpick?" Polanski asked from the open doorway to the tent.

Stonewall hefted the finely honed assegai, admiring again its graceful lines and efficient killing design. "It's the nearest thing I have to a sword. I can use this better, too. What's got me, though, is this horseback nonsense. I haven't ridden a horse since I was a kid in Texas."

"The body always remembers, Cap'n. Couple a minutes and you'll be ridin' like General Custer."

"Custer got his ass wiped."

"Sure did. An' that's what you gonna do to that wild-eyed little camel-humper out there. We'd better get goin', it sounds like they're ready."

"What's the proper wearing apparel for one of these?"

"Seems like they did it bare-assed at one time, if I recall correctly. But now I'd say no shirt would be fitting. Besides, your hairy chest will put him at a psychological disadvantage."

Two fine, spirited Arabian stallions had been led before the small canopied platform where Sharif Mammaudz sat with his family. The Tuareg leader, whose neatly trimmed beard was flecked with strands of gray, had eleven sons, ranged in age from seven to twenty-five, two wives and five daughters, with Najid the oldest. Flags and banners had been erected and fluttered in the light afternoon breeze. Stonewall, accompanied by Polanski, walked to a place near the edge of the podium and saluted the Sharif.

"I'm ready for whatever comes next, Your Excellency."

"Good. You have prepared yourself with weapons with which you are familiar. Wise planning. You may have your choice of mounts. When Ali Hammad arrives, the contest can begin."

Stonewall selected the gray, instead of the sorrel stallion. He looked quick on his feet and strong in the shoulders. When Ali Hammad al Taliq strode cockily from his tent, the Sharif gave a signal to the man who would judge the contestants, his chief scout, Abu Bakr Hamza. Hamza stepped forward and handed each man a long, thin Tuareg lance. His puckered, prune face betrayed no emotion but his dark eyes flickered hate at Stonewall. He raised his hands for silence and spoke loudly enough for everyone to hear.

"The first trial will be with the lance. Each warrior must pull from the ground as many of ten stakes as he can. They must be securely driven onto the lance point and come free of the ground. Ali Hammad shall go first."

Casting a defiant sneer at Stonewall, Ali Hammad rode to the starting point. He poised himself in the saddle and waited. An ancient, brass flintlock rifle of Moorish design fired in a cloud of gray powder smoke and Ali Hammad drove his heels into the Arab's ribs. The stallion bolted forward.

Down went the lance tip. Ali Hammad lined up on the first target and speared it neatly. Then the second, third, fourth, fifth and sixth. His horse missed a stride in the ten paces separating number six from seven and Ali Hammad failed to take it from the ground. He easily speared the remaining three, amid wild cheers from his fellow tribesmen.

"You are next, Mr. Stonewall," the Sharif announced in a soft baritone. "And may Allah give you good fortune."

Stonewall rode into the line with the remaining stakes and experimentally dipped the lance point. He adjusted his position in the saddle and tightened his grip on the long wooden shaft, couched under his right arm. Again the antique smokepole bloomed greasy smoke and boomed its challenge.

Too soon! Stonewall's body swayed when the stallion leaped forward and he missed the first stake entirely.

88

The second broke off at ground level, leaving him zero for two. At least he had the range, he thought to himself. The third stake splintered and came free, stuck fast to the lance point. Now the fourth.

The fifth.

Sixth. Hell, this was getting easy.

He lost the seventh and recovered on numbers eight and nine. Ten refused to come free of the sandy soil and nearly unhorsed him.

Ali Hammad al Taliqu had clearly emerged the victor.

Both opponents trotted back to the platform and halted in front of the Sharif. Willing hands relieved them of the lances. Ali Hammad drew his sword, a long, curved blade, single-edged affair with intricate scroll-work engraving. Stonewall slid the assegai from its bull-hide sheath.

"The second contest will be against the Invincible Warrior," Hamza announced. Immediately the teen-ager began to spin the arm with its dangerous spiked ball. Once more, Ali Hammad went first.

On his initial pass he crowded the crossarm too much and was forced to duck to avoid being struck. He managed only a weak, ineffective slash at the straw padded chest. His face contorted with self-disgust and anger, he rode silently back to the starting line. The old timer with the brass muzzle-loader blasted away with his piece and Ali Hammad streaked down the field.

His sword arm flashed up and he parried the oncoming bludgeon. Ali Hammad twisted in the saddle, once beyond the crossarm and delivered a long, ripping slash to the padded back that laid it open, spilling straw onto the ground.

The crowd bellowed their approval. Ali Hammad's boyish, Anglo features twisted into a smug sneer when he rode to the improvised grandstand. A small sickle-shaped scar on his left cheek stood out whitely against his light olive skin.

"I have already won," he announced arrogantly to Stonewall, when the soldier of fortune started toward the take-off point.

"Don't hold your breath, you little pig fucker." An angry man made mistakes, Stonewall knew. He wanted to provoke Ali Hammad into recklessness. He raised the assegai above his head to signal readiness and in a second bolted down the rutted path toward the swinging arm. At the last instant, he cut to the right, ahead of the onrushing ball of poisonous date palm thorns and ran in front of the straw man.

With calm deliberation, Stonewall drove the tip of his assegai deep into the padded front piece and gashed upward. Straw boiled out in a flurry. Still maintaining his distance from the threatening mace, he turned to his left in the saddle and swung his blade once more.

A loud pop sounded when the assegai severed the top of the post and sent the stuffed head flying.

"*Ulh-ulh-ulh-ulh-ulh!*" Loud shouts of approval rose from the spectators. Small boys raced out to touch Stonewall's legs and pat his horse. They formed an honor guard that escorted the soldier for hire back to the platform.

"What's next," he asked cockily.

"Two races, to prove mastery over the horse," Sharif Mammaudz informed him. "First you must do vaults on and over the running horse, then you will use a pair for a Roman race."

"Oh, hell, I never could stand up on a horse's back."

Two young men held a length of rope to indicate the starting gate. Stonewall held back so he could study his opponent's technique. Confidently, Ali Hammad rode into place and nodded to indicate he was ready.

In three lengths, the sorrel stallion reached a full gallop. Ali Hammad freed his feet from the stirrups and swung his agile, muscular young body out of the saddle. He scissored his legs, dropped to the left until his feet touched the ground, then hurtled through the air, over the heaving back of his mount and repeated the performance on the right side. He made three similar vaults, then headed back toward the mass of the crowd. In one hand he held a coil of rope. When he neared the spectators, he pivoted in the saddle and leaped over the drumming back hoofs of the Arabian.

On the ground he let the lead rope play out and directed the animal into a circle. Now he did standing leaps that put him astride, then over the other side and under the horse's neck. He executed a rearward vault, often called a Trooper's Mount, as a finale. His fellow Tuaregs roared their approval.

Stonewall looked grim, his face lined with concentration. How could he follow an act like that? He urged his mount into position. The sturdy steed trembled with anticipation. Stonewall gigged him at the starting signal and raced down the wide field.

He tried a tentative swing to the left. It worked. Quickly he began to unwind in a twisting, sinuous series of swinging exercises that wound him around and over the horse. Although exciting to watch and execute, Stonewall's timing and grace lacked much that Ali Hammad had in his performance. The judge, Abu Bakr Hamza awarded credit for the contest to al Taliq. Cheers and loud applause gave approval to his decison.

Two pair of unsaddled horses were brought forward then. Stonewall eyed them with dubious enthusiasm. He mounted one animal, rose to his feet and cautiously extended one leg until he stood on the backs of both. Ali Hammad did the same, with ease and practiced skill. Slowly, Stonewall walked his team to the starting line. His knees felt weak and his sense of balance became disoriented with each step of the unshod hoofs.

"The race will be to the far pole and back, one turn of the field," Abu Bakr announced.

A booming bark of black powder set the teams in motion.

The race ended quickly, only a quarter of the way downfield. True to his prediction, Stonewall fell on his ass. He barely managed to avoid being trampled to death by his own horses.

Chagrinned, knocking dust from his trousers and feeling the salt-smart of sweat in three large sand-scraped patches on his shoulders, Stonewall walked back to the platform.

"Any more like that and I'm willing to take a dive," he confided to Polanski.

"I hear this wrestling match is no holds barred. Only thing is you can't kill the little creep."

"That works two ways, you know. Might as well get it over with."

Stonewall squared off with al Taliq and flexed his already strained muscles. The signal to start was given and Ali Hammad charged in a blind rush. Stonewall simply avoided his opponent with a back-pivot. When Ali Hammad rushed past, Stonewall clubbed him in one kidney.

Ali Hammad's face plowed up sand for only a second before the young man leaped to his feet and charged once more. This time he came in low, in a diving tackle.

At the last moment, Stonewall leaped into the air and came down hard in the middle of Ali Hammad's back. The young Tuareg's rib cage compressed and a rib bone snapped. He grunted out the air in his lungs and fought to breathe in. Stonewall maintained his position, though to everyone it was obvious the battle was over.

"They now stand even in their accomplishments," Abu Bakr Hamza announced to the Sharif. "If they embrace as brothers, the matter is settled."

"No!" Ali Hammad spat out. "I demand a duel. It is my right. A duel to first blood."

"Oh, shit. Better make this fast, feller. I'm running out of steam," Stonewall commented silently, more to himself than Ali Hammad.

"It is not customary," Sharif Mammaudz began. "An accident could happen, one of you killed. All for nothing."

"It is my right. This American profanes our world and way of life. I can not be reconciled with him. A duel, let us duel now."

Mammaudz sighed heavily. "Very well. What weapon do you choose?"

Stonewall produced a wicked smile. "I'll use my assegai."

Quickly Abu Bakr explained the rules. "You will fight without armor or shield. The first to draw blood satisfies the issue. There is to be no attempt, absolutely no attempt to kill. You will commence when I give the word and you will stop immediately when I order it. Take your positions."

Now Stonewall had two problems. The assegai had been designed to kill, not to wound. And, from the wild glint in Ali Hammad's eye, he knew the young Tuareg had every intention of killing him if he could. He walked to the place indicated by Abu Bakr and braced himself.

"Ready," the chief scout barked. "Begin!"

Eagerly, but with the cautious skill of great experience, Ali Hammad leaped forward in a vicious attack. He forced Stonewall to retreat before the forceful weaving of his long, curved sword. The tip danced before the soldier of fortune's eyes, then darted toward his bare chest.

Sparks flew when Stonewall parried with the flat of his assegai. Immediately he feinted to the right and swung the Zulu blade toward Ali Hammad's exposed ribs.

Ali Hammad recoiled from contact at the last moment. In so doing, he lost his footing and staggered to his left. At once, Stonewall moved in. He wielded the assegai with practiced ease, pressing his opponent, forcing retreat. Ali Hammad's tactics became purely defensive. Sweat began to run on his young face and a look of grim resignation replaced his earlier glow of triumph. Stonewall's stabbing spear became a blur of intricate movement. Ali Hammad correctly anticipated one powerful attack and moved his sword to block the blow.

Steel rang loudly in collision an instant before a loud, surprised roar rose from the spectators. Ten inches of Ali Hammad's blade lay in the dust.

Shock and confusion weakened the half-breed Tuareg. His arms sagged. In a flash, Stonewall reached out and lightly nicked Ali Hammad's right cheek with the razor edge of the assegai.

"Cease! The duel is ended. The victor . . . Stonewall!"

A tumultuous roar followed Abu Bakr's announcement.

Chapter Nine

Lt. Colonel Mustafa al Hawaadi, whose suave good looks reminded Westerners of the actor Omar Shariff, entered his office with a thunderous expression of total anger. Behind him came Boris Zmeyá of KGB.

"There *is* no explanation of how this happened. I am not offering any excuses for the conduct of our border security forces. If anything, it should be you who offers some sort of justification, Captain Zmeyá."

"Oh, how is that?" Use of his title, instead of Mister or Comrade, rankled the KGB officer. His cover, as a civil administrator for a team of scientists could be compromised by such carelessness. It did indicate, however, how disturbed al Hawaadi had become over the issue of this J.C. Stonewall.

"Our security police, the army and navy have been outfitted with the newest and most sophisticated detection equipment. Those devices were produced and provided by *your* country. Why did it fail to detect Stonewall's infiltration? Six men died for that failure. Now you expect some sort of explanation from *me* on how *we* supposedly miscarried on a simple task like eliminating one American agent."

"Stonewall is far more than a 'tool of the CIA.' Don't let the rhetoric of propaganda blind you to that fact. He is a mercenary. A highly trained, and competent, professional soldier who sells his services to the highest bidder. Where he goes, chaos usually follows for those involved in the people's struggle for liberation. It is convenient and highly useful for us to assign simple, emotion-laden labels to such as Stonewall. Particularly since the American press so eagerly grab hold of them for the sensationalist quality it adds to their writing. Intellectually lazy for the most part, they have no desire or ability to determine the truth." Zmeyá allowed himself a cynical smile.

"Besides, many of them do our bidding knowingly and willingly. You are aware of our Department of Disinformation? In the United States, it is staffed almost entirely of native Americans. Members of the party in that country, both open and covert, are childishly eager to do whatever they can to aid the world Marxist revolution. That zeal is most clearly expressed through the opinion makers of their television networks and the editorial pages of their newspapers. Without our Department of Disinformation, the number of words produced by these loyal associates of ours would be reduced by more than half," he ended smugly.

"What has that to do with the fact that Stonewall and another mercenary named Polanski have entered the country? Their purpose has been made quite clear to us. They will try to destroy this facility. What are we to do about it?"

Zmeyá spread his hands in a placating gesture. His barrel-chested, portly figure concealed the iron-hard muscles beneath his civilian suit. His broad, peasant face radiated trust and friendship. Mustafa al Hawaadi was not deceived by these qualities, though he had been placed under orders to accept advice from the Russian and he gave at least token attention to what the KGB man had to say.

"I merely wished to point out that this project is only one small part, and an insignificant one, of the general plan to destroy the capitalist West. Success or failure will have very little bearing on the overall strategy of the Soviet Union. As to dealing with Stonewall, why not send out patrols to check the various Bedouin and Tuareg camps. He has to have indigenous personnel in order to assault a well-protected complex like this. Somewhere you will find him. I assure you of that. When you do, I am confident you know how to handle the situation."

A modern Coleman lantern lighted the interior of the low, black, goat-hide tent given to Stonewall. He sat crosslegged on a pile of pillows, drawn up before a low, tarazzoin-laid table. For the hundredth time he wished for a decent field desk and civilized chair and cursed the Tuareg idea of opulent furnishings. In one hand he held a roster of the men who had volunteered to join the attack on Project *Noor Mawt*. An even dozen of them had previous military experience.

He would need four squad leaders and three competent rocket gunners with his section. With another trained man for Polanski, that left four others to bolster the squads. A sharp twinge in one calf reminded him he was nearing his thirty-fifth birthday. Old wounds and the exertions of the day added to his discomfort. He straightened his legs and stretched his arms over his head in a movement of luxuriant, feline grace. He grasped a bottle of White Label by the neck and sipped of its contents. A slight sound outside the tent drew his attention to the doorway. His free hand went to the .45 automatic lying on the table.

"May I come in?" Najid inquired in a soft voice.

"You're always welcome, pretty lady. Come in."

"Do you greet every guest with a gun in your hand?"

Stonewall glanced down. "Oh, this. I got the distinct feeling that Ali didn't take too kindly to the decision of the judge. I also feel the kid isn't all that bound by tradition that he wouldn't try for a little private revenge. Am I reading the situation wrong?"

"No. Not at all. Ali Hammad has a tragic past." Najid laughed lightly. "I know that sounds melodramatic, but it is the truth. Don't let his appearance fool you. He is thirty-nine years old, though quite childlike in his emotions in addition to his physical attributes. He came to the tribe from Benga hzi. A wandering waif about twelve years old. That was before I was born. His father was a European, an English or American soldier. When the occupation forces left, his mother turned him out. He was nineteen when I was born. He had lived with our tribe for seven years then and father sort of, ah, took him under his wing. He's never lost his hatred of Westerners, though. Americans in particular."

"Did you come to talk about al Taliq?"

"No. I came to learn more about you."

"That's encouraging."

"How do you feel . . . after what happened this afternoon?" Her direct gaze left no doubt about her meaning.

Stonewall returned the look with equal intensity. He reached out and grabbed the scotch bottle. "Risking my life always makes me horny."

A playful smile illuminated Najid's oval face. "I thought you might feel that way." One hand strayed to the top button of her white blouse.

"Would you like a drink of scotch?"

"Yes. Very much."

"Before or after?" Stonewall felt a responding surge in his groin. He slid out of the camouflage tee-shirt he wore and lay it aside.

"Both," she responded breathlessly. Hurriedly she undid the remaining buttons and shrugged out of the blouse. Firm young breasts, a creamy, olive-white in contrast to her darker face and hands, burst into view, swaying slightly, deep rose nipples standing erect in anticipation on the dark background of small, puffy areolas. While Stonewall poured scotch into plastic cups she quickly slid out of her remaining clothes.

Her slender body arrowed to delightfully flaring hips, flat, muscular belly accented by a small, indented knot, her artful navel, that poised like a tiny moon, over the sparse, silky black thatch of pubic hair that covered her passion-swollen mound. She knelt between Stonewall's legs and accepted a glass. They drank and set aside the empties.

Then Najid reached out and undid Stonewall's belt buckle. Stonewall noted with satisfaction that Najid followed the Western custom of shaving her legs. Nothing provided a bigger turnoff to him than a hairy-legged broad. His own need had become painfully insistent and he helped her remove his trousers and undershorts. Her eyes widened at the size of his thrusting organ, though it didn't deter her from her purpose for even a second.

Eagerly she bent downward, opening her mouth, to engulf his throbbing penis in moist, tingling warmth.

"Aaaaaah!" Stonewall sighed in contentment.

Najid's long, glistening black hair hung about her shoulders, swaying gently with the rhythm of her bobbing head. Stonewall leaned back and watched while she somehow managed to encompass all of him until her velvet lips nibbled at the thick base of his engorged member. Slowly, tantalizingly, she worked him up the long, pleasurable incline to completeness. With a mighty convulsion release gushed through him.

A contented little moan escaped Najid's lips when she withdrew from him. She rolled onto her back and spread her legs in wide invitation. "You're not through yet, are you?"

"Not likely," he murmured. His still-erect, wetly red penis swayed in front of him while he positioned himself between her legs. With practiced efficiency, she guided his throbbing maleness to the core of her being.

A violent shudder passed through Najid's body when Stonewall pierced the outer veils of her silky vagina. The tremors continued in near-orgasm while he slowly, inch-by-inch entered her slippery passage.

This could easily go on all night, Stonewall dimly acknowledged to himself when he felt the pulsating contractions of clever muscles that pulled him even deeper into her very existence.

Plaintive bleating from a hundred hungry goats awakened Stonewall shortly before dawn. Already the small boys of Sharif Mammaudz's encampment led their charges to graze on the sparse edibles at the oasis. Najid had left her bed over two hours before. A warm glow of contentment suffused him, though he had only three hour's sleep over the entire night. Stonewall slid into fresh trousers, picked up a towel and bar of soap and headed for the pool at the center of the camp.

At the oasis, Stonewall washed himself to the best allowed by Tuareg rules of modesty. He paused to light a Kent and inhale deeply. A soft rosé band stretched across the eastern horizon, with powder blue above it, bleeding into midnight blackness higher up the dome of the sky. Although the night's deep chill had not dissipated, a promise of day's inferno heat could he felt in a slight breeze that sprang up, rustling the long date palm leaves in sibilent nervousness. The cigarette tasted good. A gourd dipper provided him a drink from the well set aside for human consumption. He breathed deeply again and returned to his tent. All too soon it would be starting.

"All right! Fall in!" Hank Polanski, looking every bit of his nickname, Hulk, in desert camouflage fatigues, weapon and pack in place, yelled the equivalent of the age-old sergeant's command in the Tuareg dialect.

Immediately those assigned temporarily as squad leaders began shoving and cursing the men until they understood and obeyed. Polanski counted heads. He executed a sharp about face and saluted.

"Strike Force Rag Head all present and accounted for, sir."

"Knock off the cute shit, Polanski. Some of these guys might speak English. And try to remember, they are our allies."

"Yes sir."

"Very well, Sergeant," Stonewall returned, falling into the formality of running a training unit. "Have the men stand at ease."

Polanski saluted and swiveled around to face the troops. "At ease!" He marched briskly to a position at the left end of the improvised platoon and halted. Another about face put him at right angles to the men, about ten feet in front of the squad leaders.

"Men, this morning you will learn how to disassemble and assemble the Kalashnikov assault rifle, AK-Forty-seven. You will be instructed by Sergeant Polanski." Polanski barked out a translation while Stonewall paused. "Squad leaders will report to me for a briefing of the training schedule. We have less than a week to reach a state of readiness that will afford us success in an assault on the factory complex known as *Noor Mawt*." Stonewall watched carefully to see the effect the name would have on his fledgling troops.

None of the men stirred. "Breakfast will be in ten minutes. You will have half an hour. Then form up on the games field for weapons instructions. Sergeant!"

"Strike Force, atten-hut! Dis-missed!"

The familiar commands, heard in the strangely musical language of the Tuaregs sounded strange to

Stonewall's ears. He mused on it while he walked to his tent. Inside, Najid waited for him.

"I brought you breakfast."

A fragrant aroma rose from a brass pot filled, Stonewall knew, with thick, sweet coffee. A tray contained crisply baked, flaky rolls and sugared dates. Another a round of cheese and a third a steamed, delicately scented fish.

"My God, where did you come up with all this?"

"Being daughter of a Sharif has its advantages." She seated herself, invited him to join her. "Don't let it get cold. I have a feeling you will need all your strength to get those men to do what you want without a lot of mistakes."

"Why's that?"

"Tuaregs are fiercely independent people. We don't take well to regimentation. The Germans found that out in the war. Even their much vaunted *Gestapo* could not enforce Nazi will on the Tuareg. When they no longer wished to be encamped near German installations and munitions dumps, our people simply folded their tents and disappeared into the night. The regimes that have followed enjoyed even less success than the Nazis. Perhaps that is why . . ." Her eyes darted away with her words.

"What?"

"I . . . oh," Najid took a deep breath. "I don't like what you are doing. Nor why you are here."

"Can you explain that?" Stonewall's gray eyes narrowed to slits, inner fire glittering within.

"I don't mean in the same way as poor Ali Hammad. It's not your nationality or race that offends me. It's the forced obedience and robotization of men that results from military activity. Worse, some, if not a lot of Taureg young men will die so that you can conduct some mysterious purpose at this place you call Death

Light. I don't like what I can't understand. And I don't understand what I haven't been told about."

Stonewall shrugged. "I suppose there's no harm in telling you. Colonel Qaddafi and three American turn-coats, have set up a factory to produce atomic bombs."

Najid shuddered. "Then . . . that's . . . what you are here for? You are to destroy this evil place?"

"Yes. You might put it that way. Destroy it so thoroughly it can never be rebuilt and deal with those responsible for its inception."

"Will, will you assassinate Col. Qaddafi?"

"Unless he's at the site when we hit, he won't have a hair on his rotten commie head bothered by what we do. More's a pity," he added parenthetically.

"I hate war," Najid exploded vehemently between bites of fish.

"Most reasonable people do."

"I hate what it does to the men who must fight it."

Stonewall sighed. He'd heard all this too many times. "I had hoped that when your father said you were liberated by Tuareg standards, it didn't also mean you had contracted the fatal, self-destructive disease of liberalism. The world is already too full of sick-minded people running around trying to convince everyone that it is preferable, even noble, to live as slaves in an ant-hill society run by the Marxist bastards. Better Red than dead, they chant in mindless cant. Better to live as serfs in a new, perpetual Dark Ages, than die as free men. Well, I see it a bit differently. *Better dead Reds* is my slogan. I don't think I can finish them all. But I intend to get more than my share. If everyone felt and did the same we could wipe those scum off the face of the earth in less than five years." Stonewall abruptly stopped his lecturing. He took a deep breath and a long swallow of coffee.

"Wheew! Enough of soap-box time for now."

"I've never met anyone with such strong convictions. My father is close. He feels strongly about freedom for all Tuareg tribes. Not only now but guaranteed for all time. He also thinks that our only hope of insuring that is to tend more closely to allegiance with the West. Somehow you made it seem so hopeless, foredoomed to conquest by the East. Is there no hope?"

"Don't ask me that. I can't give you an honest answer. I don't think so. I don't want to believe there isn't. Yet, so long as venal politicians have their hand out for more graft, more votes from this or that racial or ethnic group and cynically take money from their country's enemies to influence the direction of government, how the hell can a mere soldier do anything about stopping the eventual decay and dissolution of Western civilization? Oh, hell, let's get off this subject. The food was great, last night was terrific and I have a long day ahead of me."

"I think I'm in love with you, Stonewall."

"Naw, that isn't love. That's post coital contentment."

Five minutes later Sharif Achmed Mammaudz entered Stonewall's tent. "I've come to speak to you about this impending raid. Mr. Kurin's representative in Tripoli has given me to understand that the facility you are to attack is one for making atomic weapons that will be used against your country."

"Yes, sir, that is correct."

"We do not like the current government. Nor do we recognize the so-called nation of Libya. All of the desert, from Morocco to the Nile, is our ancestral heritage. Artificial borders, enforced by guns and airplanes, are only a transitory state. The desert is eternal. Against its implacable existence, all things crumble and fade away.

"Until recently, the Italians were here. Before them, two thousand years ago, the Caesars strode through their fine villas, along the limestone block paved vias and watched bloody contests in their arenas. Prior to that, the Carthagenians, under the powerful Barca family." The graying Sharif shook an age and hardship gnarled finger.

"All of them have passed away. Hardly anything remains above the relentless sands to mark their presence here. Man, no matter how powerful his weapons, is mortal. Muammar Qaddafi is nothing more than a petty criminal, a sneak-thief who has stolen a pseudo-country and appointed himself leader of it. He and the bandits who build these terrible bombs for him will all be rotted away in their graves and the desert will still go on. Yet, because of this, you come and ask that Tuaregs die for America."

"No, sir. I only ask that they be willing to fight and to die if necessary so that the Tuaregs will remain free men." Stonewall didn't feel the least hypocritical about what he said, not even slightly cynical.

"Explain yourself."

"What you say about Qaddafi is true. Unfortunately it doesn't go far enough. That is a superficial view. The cause that Qaddafi espouses is much bigger than Libya. The goal of the Soviet Union and all other communist countries is the conquest of the world. In every instance where they have prevailed, the rightful inhabitants of the country have been absorbed into the new Marxist slave state or ruthlessly exterminated. Hell, they're doing it right now in Nicaragua. Thousands of Indians, the native people of that country, are being slaughtered. The Spanish first discovered that they made poor slaves, so naturally they would not fit into the Marxist machine. If the ambitions of Qaddafi and his masters in Moscow go unchecked, ten years from now there won't be any Tuareg to appreciate the desert."

"How do you presume they will accomplish this?"

"You are aware of the relocation program? Also that the tribes are resisting it?" Stonewall fired his best shot. "Where do you suppose they will test these bombs before unleashing them on my country?"

Sharif Mammaudz's eyes widened and tight lines of anger formed around them, turning his craggy visage into a landscape of eroded gullies. He rose to his feet, uncrossing his legs in a graceful movement. He extended a hand to Stonewall and the light of conviction glowed in his obsidian orbs.

"Such monstrous men could destroy even the desert itself. From now on you have my unconditional support. Before, I felt this to be a mere distraction for Mr. Kurin, an international chess game to amuse a jaded millionaire oil magnate. I fear I owe him an apology. You, too, Mr. Stonewall. If there is anything you need, you have but to ask. The men will follow you without question."

"Thank you, sir. Now there is a little matter of obtaining some Soviet-made rocket launchers and ammunition."

"This afternoon," Polanski barked at his trainees, "we are going to fire the AK-Forty-seven. There are two modes of fire; semi-auto and full automatic. The first is inherently more accurate and is used against targets beyond one hundred fifty meters. The second can be applied in two ways. First as area fire to provide large volumes that will, hopefully, deny the terrain to the enemy and break his assault. This is passive and counter-productive. The only way to defeat an enemy is to take the battle to him; kill him or drive him out. To do this automatic fire is used in the assault to keep the opposing force pinned down, unable to lift their heads and blast you. It is also used to suppress fire from bunkers and machinegun nests. Such strong points have advantages that can be countered only when the volume of fire reaching them allows for close-in tactics resulting in neutralizing the installation.

"For reasons of time and ammunition accountability, you will train primarily on slow fire. You will not, I repeat, will not, unless otherwise instructed, put your piece on full auto. Before the actual assault you will all fire two magazines in the full automatic mode. Are there any questions before we go to the range?"

One eager young Tuareg raised his hand. "Trooper Salim, Sergeant. What is full automatic?"

"What is a mode, Sergeant?" another voice called out.

"Oh, Christ! Why was I blessed with this assignment?" For the next half hour, Polanski carefully detailed all the information he had painstakingly given the trainees during their morning familiarization program. Still unsatisfied, he grimly set out at the head of the column when the men marched to the improvised rifle range.

Barrrrip! Barrrip! Barrrip! A cascade of 7.62mm slugs chewed ground, sky and more ground, some flying closely in between trainees and a startled Polanski. The Hulk leaped into instant action, oblivious to the bright brass stream of ejected shell casings that assaulted his chest until he grabbed the offending AK-47 in one big fist and smashed the other into the jaw of the hapless young Tuareg who held it.

Silence fell, along with the trainee, who gingerly rubbed his jaw and looked aghast at Polanski. "I didn't know it was on full auto, Sergeant. Honestly I didn't"

"You moronic son of a she-camel and a goat, pig head, puke brain . . ." The tirade went on for several blistering seconds, concluded by Polanski throwing the AK-47 at its owner and stepping back with black disgust painted on his mobile, angry features. "You need a keeper. And I need a beer."

"Beer, Sergeant?" Polanski's striker for Assistant Platoon Sergeant inquired.

"Yeah. Beer. You know," he searched for the word. "*Tibra.*"

"Ah, *Tibra, effendi* Sergeant. We have *tibra.* There is a goatskin bag of it over under that tree cooling for your needs."

"Well, why didn't you say so? All right, ten minute break," he yelled at the astonished troops. "Smoke if you've got 'em. Me, I know what I'm gonna do."

Chapter Ten

Although Moslem, the Tuaregs did not strictly adhere to that religion's prohibition of alcohol. Much to his delight, Polanski found the local equivalent of beer much to his liking. In early evening, Stonewall went looking for the retired sergeant major and found him in his tent with a skin full, both goat and human, of the Tuareg brew. Polanski was in the process of teaching some of the young desert dwellers the intricacies of draw poker. The stakes, naturally enough for Hank Polanski, were pint portions of *tibra*.

"School's out for the night, Sarge. We've got business to discuss."

"Oh, hell, Cap'n. I was just beginnin' to win."

"I'll bet you were." Stonewall took a seat on one of the inevitable piles of pillows. He lifted the bottle of White Label to his lips and let a long, pale amber stream flow down his throat. Satisfied for the moment, he flicked the pink tip of his tongue over the residual wetness.

"You have 'em on the rifle range again in the morning," he began. "In the afternoon we're supposed to start rehearsals on the assault. Damnit, I wish Phil Nichols had made it here in time. We have nothing factual to go on."

"A perimeter is a perimeter. We can start with that."

"You're a genius, Polanski. What else can we do?"

"When will this Nichols be here?"

"In three or four days. He wanted to verify some last minute details."

"Christ, there's a limit to how long we can remain in-country, even in a fucking desert, without being discovered."

"There's not much chance of that, at least not a recon in force finding us. The Tuaregs move around a lot and not on any predictable schedule or route. What bothers me about the time factor is that Qaddafi's assholes might finish those fucking bombs and start putting them to use before we can make the raid. If that happens, we're all in deep shit."

"Left! Move left, damnit!" Polanski shouted at one trainee. He and his section practiced taking out a machine-gun installation. Their rifles were empty, the knives real enough and rocks simulated handgrenades. Since the simulation involved infiltrating a perimeter, the killing was supposed to be done quietly. On the far side of the training ground, Stonewall led another group through a similar exercise. Polanski wondered how well it was going. He looked to his right in time to see one of his men hurl a rock into the log and sand pillbox.

"Not a grenade, you idiot! It's supposed to be quiet. Use your knife."

"A rock is a rock, Sergeant," came the laconic reply. "I hit the guard in the head with a rock."

Polanski groaned. Would they ever learn? It only added to his personal agony. Unlike beer, *tibra* tended to give him a nasty head. He had discovered that fact early in the morning.

A whistle shrilled and the Tuareg troops melted into the sand. The camp crier set up a wail about visitors and in the distance Polanski could hear the roar of approaching engines. Half a minute later Stonewall slithered up to him, negotiating the open expanse in near-invisibility.

"What's the score?"

"Don't know, Cap'n. Somebody coming."

Two jeeps and a three-quarter ton truck rolled into the oasis. Military markings stood out clearly on their bumpers. A lean young man, in an officer's uniform, stood in the lead vehicle and barked a question in Arabic. His tone held all the rank arrogance of one who thought himself infinitely superior to those he addressed. No one answered the query.

"Are the Americans, Stonewall and Polanski, in this encampment?" he repeated. No one stirred, no one replied. "May Allah curse you all. Insolent slugs, answer me! Are the Americans here?" The crowd parted suddenly.

"There are no *farangi* here, American or otherwise," Sharif Achmed Mammaudz announced in a steely voice.

"I can not accept your assurances of that. We must search the camp."

"That would be a violation of hospitality," the Sharif responded simply.

"Do not interfere, old man, or you will get a bullet for your efforts. We represent the People's Army of the Revolutionary Command Council. To disobey our orders is an act of treason."

"We recognize no authority over us by the Revolutionary Command Council. We are free men, Tuaregs, responsible only to Allah."

"Don't argue philosophy with me, you old fool. What do you know of such things? Liberty comes only from Colonel Maummar al Qaddafi. 'Freedom—Socialism—Unity.' What is your name?" he snapped after his flourish of Marxist zeal.

"I am Sharif el *Hadj* Achmed Mammaudz of the al Hamdillah Tuaregs," Achmed responded with pride.

For a moment the officer seemed taken aback. "A *Hadj?* You? You have been to Mecca? I doubt that. Where is your green turban cloth?"

"It is not traditional among the Tuareg nobility to wear the color green. But the banner flies over my tent." The Sharif gestured toward his goat-hide dwelling.

"Well then, Oh *Hadj*, step aside and let a humble

111

soldier of the Revolutionary Command Council get on with his duties."

"Soldier is it? You are *shurtah* or I am an infidel," Achmed growled. Then he stepped into the press of his people with an elaborate gesture, bowing deeply at the waist and making a flourish with one arm. "But your men have the guns. Go ahead, lap dog of Ali Jadi," he concluded, naming the current Minister of the Interior and Director-General of Public Investigations.

The officer stiffened, though he made no reply. He turned to his men. "Search the tents."

Uniformed soldiers, armed with an assortment of European and Soviet weapons, jumped from the vehicles and began to approach tents. Their inspection of the camp took a long time. During their absorption with duty, Stonewall and Polanski hugged the sand.

"What happens when they find our stuff?" Polanski asked.

"Then there'll be trouble." A small boy drifted their way, walking in aimless zig-zags. When he drew near, Stonewall raised his head.

"The Sharif said to tell you that everything that would identify you as Americans has been well hidden," the youngster announced in a whisper.

Half an hour went by with no results. On three occasions the young officer was summoned to some suspicious tent. The last time he returned to his jeep with a dark scowl on his face. He jerked his arm in the air and his sergeant blew a whistle to summon the men. While they gathered the lieutenant twice glanced purposefully toward the training ground. When his men boarded the truck and second jeep, he climbed into the front of the lead vehicle and three engines growled to life. At a signal from the lieutenant, they started out, not away from the camp, but directly toward the training area at high speed.

"Oh, shit, someone ratted," Polanski complained, shoving a full magazine into the base of the M-14.

"Or he spotted something moving out here and guessed the rest," Stonewall amended. He had already inserted a thirty round box magazine into the Sidewinder. Now he drew back the cocking knob. The white-haired soldier of fortune sprang to his feet and swung the stubby barrel of the submachine gun in line with the advancing jeep.

"Hit it!" he yelled.

A line of .45 caliber slugs from the Sidewinder stitched spider webs across the windshield of the advance jeep. The driver and the ambitious lieutenant died instantly. The passengers in the rear dived over the side to avoid a similar fate.

A sudden loud, continuous roar from all sides brought a wild smile to Stonewall's lips. By God, those provisional squad leaders had earned their stripes! They had quietly instructed their troops to load live. Son of a bitch! They might just make it.

Stricken beyond recovery, the first jeep careened past where he and Polanski stood and smashed into a low, simulated bunker. Behind it, blood, cloth bits and flesh flew when a scything cloud of 7.62mm Soviet rounds struck it from the AK's in the hands of green troops. Not so damn green, Stonewall corrected himself when he saw the result.

He snapped off a pair of three round bursts into the radiator and windshield of the onrushing three-quarter ton truck. Besides him, Polanski methodically ticked off five shot rips from the M-14 on full auto that blasted bullets into metal, canvas and mortal human tissue inside the small conveyance. Their target canted on one blown-out tire and tottered onto the passenger side. It slithered along the sand for a moment, then lay still. Immediately, return fire came from the soldiers trapped in the rear.

Stonewall and Polanski leaped apart, rolled and came up blazing at the enemy. Suddenly Bashir Fawzi appeared at Stonewall's side, his AK-47 spitting death at Qaddafi's security police. Stonewall gave him a brief grin of battle confidence and rushed forward a dozen yards, his movement covered by quick chatter from the Sidewinder.

Men screamed and died while Stonewall ran across the ground toward the overturned truck. He fitted a new magazine into the well of the Sidewinder and knelt briefly to aim a burst at the driver, who labored to free himself from the warped door.

The soldier-policeman's arms flew wide, one crashing through the shattered windshield, a Makarov pistol clutched in dead fingers. Figures of the Pathet Lao appeared on the screen in Stonewall's mind and the blood lust rose to a humming pitch. He wanted to get in close, spill blood and guts on the ground and watch these communist slime die with horror imprinted on their faces.

"Yeeeaaahhooo!" he bellowed his eerie rebel yell and charged in on the truck, sub-gun forgotten, his assegai flashing out into the afternoon sun. The first Libyan to encounter that deadly Zulu blade died without time to know how he had been killed. Stonewall turned on another desert louse who stumbled over the sand, favoring a wounded thigh.

"La', la'!" the fancy-uniformed communist screamed when he saw Stonewall rushing toward him. "No!"

"Hell yes!" Stonewall snarled when the tip of the assegai bit into flesh in the man's tender abdomen.

Steel sliced through muscle, cleaved apart coils of intestine and sent a fountain of blood gushing out. Stonewall jerked backward in time to avoid the crimson tide. The body, an empty sack, plopped on the ground. A grenade crashed on Stonewall's left.

Slivers of shrapnel whizzed through the air above the soldier for hire's head and he directed his attention to the rear of the truck, where three survivors fought valiantly against the overwhelming force of Tuareg firepower. With speedy stealth, Stonewall approached from their blind side.

"Hey! Qaddafi sucks camel dick!" Stonewall shouted at their surprised backs. He had Polanski drill him in how to deliver the epithet in Arabic until he had it exact. His ploy worked perfectly.

The first soldier turned toward him. The assegai whistled through the air.

The Libyan desert louse's body continued to turn, cut free from his head by a vicious swipe of the assegai that had severed muscle and neck bones. His gaping mouth chewed sand a moment later. The ragged stump released a twin geyser of blood above the still erect cadaver. Pressing the advantage of his surprise attack, Stonewall lunged forward and buried his blade to the hilt in the armpit of the second *shurtah* paramilitary-policeman. His left hand suddenly filled with his .45 automatic.

Three slugs smacked into the remaining Libyan. He jerked and twitched with each impact like a demented puppet. Then Allah cut the strings and he fell in a boneless sprawl. Broad patches of red stained the back of his uniform shirt. Stonewall spun to confront another enemy.

He encountered only silence.

A minute. Less than one fucking minute, Stonewall thought, and fifteen Libyans died. Pride in the men he would be fighting with swelled his chest.

"Keep away from me, you fascist pig! Don't touch me, imperialist lackey!" a near-hysterical feminine voice shrilled in English from behind Stonewall. The white-haired soldier of fortune whirled and dog-trotted to the point where the passengers had unassed the doomed jeep.

"Who have we got here?" he inquired when he came up to Polanski and three of the Tuareg squad leaders. He examined their surprise package. She wore a tan safari shirt and matching short pants, the pockets bulging with well-formed breasts and pencils. Knee-high socks of the same color rose from cordovan Wellingtons that fit small feet. Her soft brown hair was cut mannishly short and her yellow eyes, flecked with ochre slivers, flashed with maniacal hatred.

"Beats me, Cap'n."

"Another CIA mercenary assassin," she spat at Stonewall. "Keep your hands off me, too."

Stonewall uttered a harsh bark of laughter. It startled the woman, girl really, and calmed her. Only for a moment. His words sent a 220 volt current of fury through her slender, broad-hipped body.

"Goddamn, lady. You sure have that trite Marxist jargon down pat. I gotta hand it to you. Now, who the fuck are you?"

"You'll find out soon enough. When I write up what happened here this afternoon, the whole world will know about you murdering, racist stormtroopers."

A big hand streaked from Stonewall's side. His thick, muscular fingers bit painfully into the young woman's upper arm and he hauled her roughly to her feet. He jerked her back and forth like a terrier worrying a rat.

"I asked your name. Are you going to give it to me or do I turn you over to my Tuaregs to torture an answer out of you?"

Stonewall's words sobered the girl. She struggled to gain her composure. "I am Melissa Gould. I'm a reporter for *Newspeak*. Even an illiterate minion of the CIA must have heard of our newsmagazine," she added defiantly.

"Oh, that Red rag. Sure. I use it to line my cat box. Do

you mind telling me what you were doing out here with Qaddafi's *Gestapo?*"

"I mind a great deal being in the clutches of a notorious mercenary, a killer of women and children. You are J. C. Stonewall, aren't you?"

"I am. Only I don't kill women and children. I leave that for your terrorist buddy, Qaddafi and his asshole pal, Yassir Arafat. Also get one other thing straight. I am not a mercenary. I am a professional for hire. There's a big difference."

"I expected some sort of self-justifying bullshit from you, Stonewall. I'm immune to your lies, though. I've seen photographs, talked to survivors now living at the old royal palace as guests of Colonel Qaddafi. Even a child could see through your half-witted deception."

"You're in a bad position to be running your smart-ass mouth, Melissa. I asked you a question and you haven't answered it yet."

"Ms. Gould," she icily corrected. "I came here to do a story on the valiant struggle Col. Qaddafi is making against the ruthless oppression of our fascist president and the administration. I learned from a reliable source that you and this other CIA cretin had entered the country illegally for the purpose of assassinating Col. Qaddafi and important members of the government."

"Bullshit! I am a private citizen, hired by a private citizen to dispose of a particularly dangerous situation that you should learn a little more about before swallowing wholesale all the sugar-coated crap Qaddafi's Marxist chums are putting out."

Self-righteous fire radiated from Melissa's yellow eyes. "Then you admit you are here to committ murders for the CIA!"

"I don't work for the CIA and my main job isn't to kill any Libyans if it can be prevented. You don't listen too well. It must be all that Red garbage stuffed between

117

your ears, interferes with the hearing process. Are you aware that the 'valiant' madman you heap so much praise on is in the process of building atomic bombs, to sneak them into the States and set them off in a demand for our surrender?"

Melissa blinked. "I don't believe it. Even if it were true, I say, good. America deserves that sort of punishment for its long record of violating human rights and oppressing the freedom-loving peoples of the world."

Livid with fury, Stonewall struggled to restrain his impulse to drive a hard-knuckled fist into the gloating face of this communist-loving creep. "You're insane, *Ms.* Marxist Gould. You're even more fucking nuts than that bloodthirsty bastard Qaddafi." To Polanski he growled, "Take the prisoner away. See that she's tied securely and confined under heavy guard."

"Prisoner? You can't take me prisoner. I'm a member of the working press. I have international credentials," she spluttered. She jerked away from Polanski's restraining hand and faced Stonewall, glowering, fists on hips.

"I don't give a fuck what you are, *Ms.* Gould." Stonewall made the pseudo-word sound like the buzzing of a drunken bee. "Right now you are our prisoner, until we figure out what to do with you. If you don't like it, take it up with the Minister of the Interior. Meanwhile, keep that puerile Marxist crap you're spouting to yourself and stay off my ass."

Stonewall turned and angrily strode away.

Chapter Eleven

"We have no other choice, Achmed," Stonewall argued to the Sharif half an hour later. "Those desert lice must have radioed their position to someone before they drove in here."

"That may be so. Provided there is another unit close enough to be contacted. Remember, we are hundreds of kilometers into the desert."

"True enough, but we can't take the chance."

"Moving a tribe of this size is a major undertaking. Water must be scouted, if we take an unfamiliar track, and food for the trek prepared in advance for both men and animals."

"I understand your problem, Achmed, really I do." Stonewall took a long pull from the mouth of a bottle of White Label. "And I sympathize. But the bottom line is this. Even if they failed to reach their headquarters or another roving patrol, when they don't come back, someone's coming looking for them. We can't afford to compromise this mission on an off-chance that whoever conducts that search will miss our location."

Achmed Mammaudz sighed heavily. "I will issue the necessary orders immediately. Now, there is another matter. The American reporter. What do you intend doing with her?"

"What would you suggest?" Stonewall countered rhetorically. "We can't let her go. She'd streak back to Benghazi and tell Muhammad Ali Jadi exactly where we are and what we're up to. That would bring down an air strike that would cream us before we had a chance to hit the factory."

119

"I don't know about you, but mad as she makes me, I don't like the idea of killing her," he concluded.

"The only alternative you leave is totally unacceptable."

"What's wrong with taking her with us?"

"She's a fuckin' pain," Polanski growled from where he sat in the Sharif's tent, sipping on a large goatskin of *tibra*.

"Sergeant Polanski is correct, if a bit graphic. It would require men detailed to guard her and thus unable to help with our move. Also women to prepare food. If she can't be trusted to fend for herself, she should be disposed of."

"If she goes along, with or without her cooperation, it might open her eyes to the fact that not everyone is in love with that son of a bitch Qaddafi. She's full of bluster and bullshit right now, but if she saw what's going on with her own eyes and touched a real atomic bomb, held it in her hands, there's no telling how much mileage we could get out of that."

"Take her all the way to the objective?" Polanski blurted. "Have you gone bonkers, Cap'n? No fucking way. No. That's crazy talk. I say waste her little Red ass and leave her for the vultures."

"You gonna pull the trigger, Sergeant?"

Polanski swallowed *tibra*. He belched loud and long. "Ain't my fucking job."

"It is now. As of this minute. We decide to terminate her, frag her ass, and you blow her away." He turned back to the Sharif. "I still say we take her along."

"Such a course is filled with danger."

"So's living in fucking Qaddafi's Libya, Achmed. What more risk is it? Well?"

Achmed Mammaudz sucked the juice from a rosy plum. He drew smoke from an ornate glass and silver hookah through the long hose and into his mouth. At last he shrugged. "Your logic overwhelms me, Stonewall. All right. I agree to take her along."

"Hank?" Stonewall inquired, using the sergeant major's first name in a personal appeal to reconciliation.

"Awh, shit. If I know you, you probably want to crawl into her pants. Okay by me. Just one more fucking detail to take care of."

Wild Tuareg music squealed and thumped through the camp. The night came alive with bonfires. Men, women and laughing, shouting children drifted from one bright spot to another. They sampled a bit of *couscous* here, some crispy roast goat there, fragrant, mouth-cooling mare's milk from another friend. Sharp, curved knives sliced into dung-cured rounds of creamy cheese and a cluster of devotees gathered around an freshly uncapped skull to partake of their favorite dish, puddled goat brains. Everywhere skins of *tibra*, cooled in the dark recesses of the well, passed from hand to hand. On the edge of all this celebration, Abu Bakr Hamza spotted one glum, distorted face.

"Peace be with you, Ali Hammad al Taliq," he greeted the unhappy-looking half-breed.

"And Allah's peace be with you, Abu Bakr Hamza."

"You are not celebrating with the rest?" Abu Bakr tossed off casually.

"I find no cause to celebrate. We must move, yet this is the richest oasis in our lands. And why? Because some Libyan soldiers have stupidly been killed."

Abu Bakr placed an arm around Ali Hammad's shoulders and led the younger man out into the dark outer edges of the oasis. "Which is the exact reason for the festivities. Ah, that was a great victory the American led our men to, was it not?" Abu Bakr felt Ali stiffen under his grasp at mention of the battle. "Ah-ha! Do I detect the cause of your discomfort? Is it the American, Stonewall?"

"It is *any* American," Ali Hammad cried in frustration. "Cursed be all their names!"

"My, such vehemence. Tell me, I nor anyone has ever pried before, why do you hate the Americans so implacably?"

"Rather, go and ask my whore of a mother."

"Oh?"

Ali Hammad pulled free of Abu's grasp and faced the older man. A trembling coursed through his lean, muscular frame and Abu Bakr thought that, for a glimmer of a moment, tears shone in the eyes of the boyish-looking Ali Hammad. He clenched teeth and fists to regain control before answering.

"It is an old story. From long ago. In the great war when the *tedesci* and Italians fought the English. Then . . . the Americans came." Such bitterness crept into Ali Hammad's voice that it prompted Abu Bakr to couch his next question in tones of sympathetic understanding.

"It has to do with your father, does it?"

"That swine and son of a swine!" Ali Hammad cursed in Arabic. "Yes. He was an American soldier. He met my mother. They became . . . lovers. Then my mother became pregnant. They never married, though he claimed he wanted to. Oh, everything was fine while the Americans remained in Benghazi. Then they sailed across the Mediterranean to Sicily. I was born just before the Feast of Ramadan in nineteen forty-four. Shortages had already begun.

"My mother could get no help from the neighbors. They shunned her because she had slept with one of the foreigners. I remember always being hungry. In two years, when I was six and seven, I grew only one centimeter. My belly stuck out and so did my ribs. A strong wind would blow me off my feet. Other children made fun of me. Even more so because I . . ." Ali Hammad's shame caused him to blush so deeply that Abu Bakr

122

could see the dark stain even in the stygian night.

"My father, whom my mother blindly loved until the day she died and obeyed without question in all things, had insisted that I not be circumcized. I had to live with that blot until I came to the al Hamdillah Tuaregs. The Imam at Tazerbo performed the ritual on my thirteenth birthday. The shame of this, and the pain caused by the operation at such a late age, made me shy. I never sought out girls. I have never . . . had a woman."

"Boys?"

Ali Hammad nodded. "Many times when I was little. And in my youth. I was a novelty. Those already inclined that way found me, ah, intriguing. We were so poor, you see, and I quickly accepted that as an easy way to make a few piasters. When I was eight, my mother died. For the next four years, until I ran away from Benghazi, I sold my body to survive. Among my customers were a few Americans. Tourists who wanted to see where their soldiers had fought during the war.

"One of them, a smiling, soft-spoken bald man with a fringe of graying hair, wanted to take me home with him. At the last minute he must have lost his nerve. He left in the middle of the night, after putting a stack of hundred piaster notes beside me in the bed. That's the money I used to escape."

"I see. Another American deserting you. Do you have a lover now?"

"No. I haven't allowed myself to indulge in sex for many years. Nearly twenty, in fact."

"You must suffer."

A sob of desperation wrenched from Ali Hammad's tormented throat. "That is why it is unforgivable for this American, Stonewall to be here. I worked and struggled so hard to overcome my past, to become strong and courageous, a true Tuareg. Then, then he arrives and in one day destroys my manhood, my valor, steals my honor by shaming me in front of my tribe."

Abu Bakr felt moved to protest. "That is not so. No one laughs at you or behind your back. You out did him in horsemanship. Held your own in the skills of a warrior. An unlucky twist of the ankle cost you the grappling match. No. Do not think badly of yourself, Ali Hammad al Taliq."

"Why not? I failed my tribe and myself. Bested by an American," he made the word sound poisonous. "He must die because he is an American. He is all Americans."

"Who have always hurt you. Were there other times the Americans caused you disgrace or embarrassment?"

"As you know, I left the tribe only once, in nineteen sixty-two to work on the new American base. They refused me, said I was too young, too small, they wouldn't believe me when I told them I had an American father."

"And to you, all of this is centered in Stonewall?"

"Yes!" the word hissed out.

Abu Bakr placed a calming hand on the younger man's shoulder. "Ali Hammad you are indeed a man wronged. What you have told me has moved me greatly. I am inclined to take your side in this. There is a chance, though a slim one at the present, that should Stonewall prove to be less than beneficial to the al Hamdillah, or if he heaps more insult upon you, I might be moved to aid you in your determination to eliminate him. Go now and get a good sleep, for you see, you have friends in places you would never suspect."

Sputtering, Stonewall spat out the mouthful of scotch he had used to rinse his teeth. To think, when he had been a kid they had scotch, bourbon and rye flavored toothpaste. A novelty that had, thankfully, never caught on. After a party like the one thrown in the Tuareg camp the previous night, the taste of his favorite booze left a lot to be desired. He pulled on his tee-shirt and fatigue jacket amid an intense early morning bustle.

All around, Tuareg women struck tents and rolled them into bundles to transport on the tribe's herd of camels. Najid arrived with a breakfast tray while Stonewall zipped up his age-worn jump boots.

"Where will you be riding in the caravan?" she inquired.

"I'm not. I'm going to Tripoli to see why Phil Nichols is being held up."

"Then I'm going with you."

"No you're not."

"The whole country is looking for you. Alone you would stand out in the crowded streets of Tripoli."

"Bashir is going with me. I don't know what we might run into. To take you along is out of the question."

"To the contrary. The police will be looking for one man alone or two foreigners. I can provide protective coloration. Besides, it will give us a chance to spend some time together," Najid ended mischieviously.

"Now, that's the one argument that can win me over. Be ready in an hour." Stonewall hummed scraps of a nameless tune while he finished his preparations. Then he went in search of Polanski.

"Keep them busy," he began his instructions to the former Special Forces sergeant major. "They did a great job yesterday, but that isn't the whole war. I'll link up with you in about four days. By then they should be nearly ready and, hopefully, we'll know where our target is located."

"Right, Cap'n. There were two RPG's in that three-quarter. Neither one got messed up in the crash. That'll increase our odds a little."

"Good. Use one to train the men on. I'll take the other along in case of trouble. And get some patrols out to locate more rockets."

"Between trainin' and sneak and peek operations I'm gonna be busier than a one-armed towel boy in a Phoenix City whorehouse," Polanski complained.

"Work is good for the soul."

"I thought that was prayer."

"Well, then, let us prey a little." Stonewall walked toward the waiting jeep, accompanied by Polanski's agonized groan. The burly sergeant major had no appreciation for puns.

Stonewall's prediction of search activity came true an hour after they left camp.

A low flying, high-wing aircraft approached the jeep from the north paralleling the dusty track. When the spotter saw the vehicle, he instructed the pilot to drop down toward the ground. Stonewall identified the airplane as a Citabria, a fabric-covered ship that resembled an overgrown Piper Cub. It circled the speeding car three times, keeping pace by a bit of tricky flying.

"We're in for it now," he told Najid and Bashir. "They'll call for the closer inspection."

"There is no other roadway, *effendi* Stonewall," Bashir announced gravely. "If they send soldiers we have no way to evade them."

"Then we'll blow them away," Stonewall declared simply.

Above his head, the Citabria banked sharply to the left and flew away. The miles churned under their wheels. Without a governor on the engine, the jeep managed a respectable seventy. The Libyan manner of handling their suspicious presence in an area where a patrol disappeared came to them as a surprise.

A bright spot of reflected light on the far horizon rapidly grew to take the form of a *Mirage* jet. The French-made interceptor flashed over them low

126

enough that the three occupants of the jeep felt the tremendous force of its disturbance torque, created by super-sonic speed.

"Any ideas how to hide from *that?*" Stonewall asked.

"They go very fast," Bashir observed. "Do they turn quickly also?"

"No. It takes several dozen kilometers."

"Then I can outdrive it by taking to those hills over there." Bashir took one hand from the wheel to indicate their change of direction and the jeep careened wildly for a second.

"Go for it," Stonewall urged. He had little faith in this approach, though. He leaned over the seat and began to arm the RPG-24 Soviet rocket launcher. A quick glance showed him Najid's eyes wide with worry. He started to speak but his words disappeared in the roar of the jet passing them by once more.

"This time around he's going to shoot," Stonewall warned the others.

The horizon turned into a storm-tossed sea as the jeep rolled and swayed over the uneven ground. Low mounds rushed at them and soon enclosed the vehicle. A sense of security welled in the three fleeing people.

Like Nemesis the jet came back.

Bright lights flickered around the nosecone. Immediately all thoughts of security fled.

When the first 20mm projectile left the muzzle of the rotating-barrel cannon, Bashir yanked hard on the wheel. The jeep sped off at the ninety degree angle to the flight path. Unable to alter its course in under a half mile of the racing vehicle, the jet hammered by two hundred yards behind them.

The earth lurched.

Airborne, the jeep hurtled a narrow wadi and landed with a tire-punishing crunch. Once more the Mirage executed a one-eighty turn and thundered toward the target.

Damn! Stonewall thought in frustration. The fire safety catch on the RPG-24 would not throw. It was a now or be blown to pieces situation. Stonewall felt certain the pilot would not fall for their evasive tactic again.

Chapter Twelve

When the Mirage lined up its deadly nose, Bashir once again hauled on the steering wheel. This time to the right instead of the left. The pilot hadn't counted on that.

A stream of steel slugs burnt air and exploded sand in a line fifty yards behind them. A safe miss but getting closer. Suddenly the safety on the RPG-24 gave. Stonewall slapped Bashir on the shoulder.

"Hit the brakes!"

When the jeep slid to a dusty halt, Stonewall leaped from the passenger side and lined up the sight on the jet. He tracked it through its turn and mentally counted down until the bulbous nose filled the retical. Now, a solid squeeze . . .

With a whoosh, the Russian rocket left its tube. It accelerated in geometric progression as it burned its solid fuel and grew lighter in the process. A slight upward curve developed in its trajectory, then the deadly missile shrank out of sight.

A bright flash.

The air filled with bits of French aluminum and Libyan flesh. A gargantuan explosion shook the ground and rattled bones in three sets of inner ears.

"Kiss another jet good-bye, Qaddafi." To the others, Stonewall commented, "It would drive the lunatic Colonel up the wall if he knew an American blasted this one, too."

"Nice shootin' there, Pilgrim," Bashir nervously said in his John Wayne voice. "Next stop, Tripoli."

Bashir elected to continue across country to reach the

main north-south highway. It turned out to be a mistake. Their path took them into the tip of the north-eastern pointing finger of the Marzuq Sand Sea.

The jeep struggled on for an hour in four-wheel drive. Then without warning, the laboring vehicle sank axle-deep in the soft, shifting sand. Stonewall and the Tuareg driver climbed from the jeep and inspected the damage.

"Not even a bush to wedge under the wheels," Stonewall observed gloomily.

"And nothing to secure the winch cable to so we could drag our way out," Bashir lamented. "From here on we walk. We can't be far from the oasis of Al Harun. We can get transportation there."

"How? Buy it?"

"No. Steal it." Bashir shrugged at the absurdity of having to explain the obvious.

"That won't be necessary," Najid announced as she stepped from the jeep. "I brought along lots of money."

"I knew there was some good reason why we brought you along," Stonewall told her.

They began to walk. And walk.

Two large canvas water bags kept thirst at bay, but the blast furnace sun rapidly sapped their strength. An hour dragged past. Then twenty minutes more. Stonewall blinked rapidly, trying to verify what his doubting mind told him lay ahead.

"Oasis. Up ahead," he said, hoping his words would not dissolve it away.

"Ah, yes. Al Harun. Very small," Bashir informed him.

Three tired people stumbled into the shade of verdant palm trees ten minutes later. They ignored the pointed stares of a small band of Berbers camped there. Clad in the Moorish style, the fierce-looking desert horsemen formed a semi-circle around the trio when they sank to the ground with their backs against the bole of a tree.

"What are you doing here?" their leader demanded.

Najid remembered the traditional role of women in a tribal society and remained silent for once. Bashir unfolded the tale of their trek afoot and concluded with a request.

"We would like to buy some horses, if any are for sale."

The leader, who called himself Kassim, pondered a moment. "These are good horses. Much too good to be parted with in a hurry. I warn you, my Tuareg friend, they come high."

Impatient with the inevitable haggling, Najid spoke without thinking. "We can pay."

Kassim frowned. Women were expected to keep their tongues. He screwed his face into a look of serious contemplation. "One hundred pounds would not be too much," he offered.

"For all three?" Bashir inquired, enjoying the bargaining.

Kassim laughed. "Why, my little friend, that sum would not buy one."

Bashir feigned horror. "You would impoverish us? By Allah, such a price should purchase ten of your scrawny, under-fed nags."

"It is a long walk to Marzuq," Kassim stated simply.

"You can not leave us stranded on the sand sea. Where is the charity commanded by Allah for true believers?"

Hands turned palms up, Kassim sighed in regret. "It has gone the way of your automobile, I am afraid. One hundred-five pounds. Not a millieme less."

"Have you turned to banditry? Two hundred for the lot."

"A man can not make a profit if he sells too low."

"That is too much by half."

A shrug from Kassim. He rolled his thick lips until his bristling mustache undulated threateningly under his flared nose. "Two hundred twenty-five?" he offered.

"A hundred fifty!" Bashir snapped.

"Very well. You may have them for two hundred."

"Done and done."

Najid had given Stonewall a running translation of the barter and when they rose to claim their horses, he spoke softly to her. "Those two should go to work in the garment district in New York."

Before she could answer, Kassim spoke again, looking pointedly at the automatic weapons Stonewall and Bashir had slung over their shoulders. "Those are interesting weapons. Would you consider trading them both for a total of five horses?"

"Not likely, friend," Stonewall answered.

Although he could not understand the words, the meaning was clear to Kassim. When Bashir translated, his eyes narrowed to threatening pin points. "Accidents happen frequently on the sand sea. You could lose them."

"If any of these turkeys makes a move, drop to the ground," Stonewall told Najid. He slid his left hand into a baggy fatigue pocket. His fingers closed around the solid shape of a fragmentation grenade. So far it remained a stand-off.

"We will pay you the money you demand, take our horses and go," Bashir informed the chieftian in a cold, steady voice. "May the peace of Allah be with you."

"Peace be with you also," Kassim responded. His darting glance gave unspoken instructions to three Berbers.

Bashir made short work of saddling the mounts. Before he swung aboard his steed, the young Tuareg loosened one end of the Berber picket line, Stonewall noticed with approval. He gave Bashir a slight nod of acknowledgement and hoisted a leg over the back of a sleek Arabian. They rode only fifty feet from the oasis when Stonewall abruptly halted. He pulled the hand-grenade from his pocket, jerked out the pin and heaved it back toward the startled Berbers.

The blast had its desired effect. Though it killed no one, it sent the Berber horses, wild-eyed with fright, scat-tering across the sand. They yanked free of the loosened picket line and galloped off with whinnied shrieks. Kassim snatched an old Mannlicher-Carcano rifle from the awe-struck man beside him and took aim.

He never fired. A quick three round burst from Stonewall's Sidewinder crashed into his chest and turned the Berber chieftian into a bloody rag doll that violently thrashed for a few seconds while its life-fluids soaked into the powdery soil.

"Let's ride," Stonewall commanded.

At a full gallop, the trio disappeared over the rolling dunes.

Monotony. The utter sameness of sand, interrupted only occasionally by wind-rippled terraces, swallowed them. Ten miles, Bashir had guessed, remained to cover. All of it like the gritty uniformity that now em-braced their path. Lawrence, Stonewall thought to himself, must have been crazy *before* he did his number in the Arabian peninsula, not after the Turks got hold of him. A person had to be nuts to *voluntarily* go into a place like this. Time telescoped into an eter-nal, identical present.

Twenty minutes later Stonewall led the others up a long sand slope. At the crest they gazed down the in-cline to the black strip of highway. Bashir studied their surroundings.

"We have bypassed Marzuq. Shall we backtrack to get an automobile?"

"How far is the next town?"

"Shebha should be no more than forty-five

kilometers north. Marzuq is more than two hundred to the south."

"Let's push on then," Stonewall advised.

Little changed in the scenery for several miles. Gradually, though, the drifting dunes of the sand sea receded and a more open vista emerged. Scattered brush began to appear and the horses consumed the miles in an easy canter.

Najid rode beside Stonewall and frequently cast him curious glances. At last she expressed her concern. "How did you know Kassim's men were going to try to attack us?"

"Mark it up to instinct, I suppose. I didn't like his looks. He's not the first of that type I've dealt with." He tried to lighten the mood. "In America we call them used car salesmen."

"You are a strange man, Stonewall. And a marvelous lover."

"Are you looking for a return engagement right out here on the sand?"

"Not exactly, though the idea has appeal. When we get to Tripoli, though . . ." she left the invitation open.

"If we don't get some sort of vehicle soon, my ass will be too sore to do any fancy bobbing around. All I'll want to do is soak it in a tub of hot water."

"I think I can make you change your mind on that."

He gave her a long, hungry look. "Lady, I think you might at that."

"Sometimes you seem to be two people," she mused. "One is hard, brutal, coarse-talking, the other urbane and witty. Are you a university man?"

"I put in two years of college. I had a football scholars I guess you'd say I was a pretty big jock all through high school. I played baseball, football . . . basketball until I screwed up a knee."

"Where was this?"

"Tyler, Texas. Which is sort of stuck out there in the middle of nowhere. Anyway, back to my college days. I kind of liked it. I studied, took my own tests and made my own grades, good enough ones too, not like some of those animated sides of beef they call athletes. Vietnam was going on by then. A lot of the professors were always trying to get the students to demonstrate against war, even urged us to take over the administration building and burn down the ROTC center. I got tired of listening to their Red shit, popped one in his commie mouth and took off to join the army."

"Are you always that impulsive?"

"I suppose so. Since I joined on my own, I got a three year hitch, instead of two like draftees. Having volunteered, it turned out I couldn't stop there. I signed up for the airborne school and for Special Forces."

"Mr. Polanski, Hank, calls you Captain. Did you attend a military academy?"

"No, Najid. During my second tour in 'Nam I received a battlefield commission. Rare at best, they didn't hand out all that many this time around. You see, there has to be a war to have a battlefield."

"With all of that, why didn't you make a career of it?"

"I wanted to. Intended to, in fact. Then . . . something happened." Flashes of smooth, tawny thigh, winsome, smiling mouth, bold, hungry eyes exploded in Stonewall's brain. *Angelique!* And the goddamned Pathet Lao. The fucking commie slopes who had set up their post and beaten and raped the one thing of beauty and joy in his life and left the remains dangling from the stake for him to find. He'd gotten even, though, but not enough. Never enough.

Captain J. C. Stonewall gave the order that resulted in an entire village of suspected V.C. being gunned down, every last man, woman, child, cat, dog and canary. That had been long before the rabidly left press and the armchair generals back home conspired to make a scandal out of Mi Lai. They crucified Bill Calley for that one but they didn't get *him*. He'd been transferred back to the States and relegated to housekeeping duties and eventually pressured to resign his commission and leave the army. He still wanted to kill commies and that didn't stop him.

Trojan came into his life and Stonewall began his trade as a soldier for hire. He would go anywhere, any time for any amount of pay, just for the priviledge of killing more Marx-worshipping assholes. And here in Libya he had a whole country full of them. He couldn't ask for a better deal.

"What was it that changed your mind?"

"The army itself. There was a girl. We were in love. The commies in Laos killed her. I took it out on a village of Viet Cong. End of career." How simply, he mused, his happiness and anguish could be condensed into a minimal number of painless words. The dagger in his heart had made only a quarter turn this time.

"When did you decide to become a mercenary?"

"Please, don't use that word. The Grand Elector of Hesse and Saxe-Coberg-Goethe had mercenaries, men he impressed into his army and rented out to other countries. I don't even like the phrase soldier of fortune. I've yet to find a soldier who hires out his skills who has amassed a fortune. Most of us fight for ideals. And I suppose adventure."

"What about Hank? What does he fight for?

"Polanski? That's easy. Call it Mom, beer and apple pie. Mostly beer. And to keep from being bored in his retirement."

"He was in Special Forces with you?"

"Yes, but not in the same outfit. He put in thirty-five years and retired as a Sergeant-Major, E-Nine. That's enlisted grade nine, the highest there is."

"Now he fights other people's battles."

"Honey, there ain't no such thing as 'other people's battles.' They all fight their own wars, we only help them some. We're specialists, so to speak."

Up ahead, Bashir reined in sharply. When they caught up, he nodded down the macadam ribbon. "Roadblock."

"Well, Duke, it looks like we'll have to fight the Injuns to get through to Dodge City."

"Right. You give the word."

"Here's what we'll need to do . . ."

All five soldiers of the internal security force of the Directorate-General of Public Investigations peered suspiciously at the three persons approaching on horseback. Their leader, Sergeant Abodo, attired in a stiffly-starched, crisply clean, dark green uniform, stood out front of the two vehicles that formed the roadblock.

One, a large official sedan, retained traces of OD paint. It had once been a U.S. army car. The other was an oversized Land Rover in a military configuration. The four privates twitched irritably. The sun broiled them and insects that came from the irrigated fields south of Sebha stung in undiscouraged hordes. Too little traffic on this road and not enough to do. It led to boredom, which bred carelessness. For though they watched the travelers with rapt attention, none of them carried their rifles. Only Sergeant Abodo seemed business-like, one hand resting on the buttoned down flap of his pistol holster.

One of the riders, who lagged slightly behind the other two, could have been a woman. Heat ripples in the air distorted distant views and made such determinations difficult. The men in front seemed to be drifting further apart. Sgt. Abodo raised his left hand in a signal to halt.

"Your travel permits, please. What is your purpose in being on this road?"

"Here you are, Turkey," Stonewall said in English while he reached behind him. His big hand closed around the grip of the Sidewinder and he swung it out and forward. The force of his thrust caused his trigger finger to pull through to full auto.

At twelve hundred rounds a minute, the fat .45 slugs ripped Sergeant Abodo apart like a dynamited watermelon. Tiny chunks of green and red flew from his pulped chest and exploded out the back, taking along large hunks of vertebra. He danced a mortal minuet until Stonewall took his finger off the trigger. Starched and creased Sergeant Abodo might have been, but it didn't hold up the badly leaking bag of dead Red. He flopped onto the tarmac in front of his astonished underlings.

Immediately Stonewall leaped out of the saddle. From the corner of his eye he marked that Bashir had done the same as instructed. Already the young Tuareg grasped his AK-47 in both hands. A spray of 7.62mm copper bees stung the staff car. Windows disintegrated while the remaining security men made wild dashes for their weapons, their minds divided between fight and flight. Stonewall didn't give them a chance to make a decision on that one.

Neat, precise, three-round bursts from the Sidewinder sought the range. A trio of jacketed judges passed sentence on a chubby Libyan. They ruled his left kidney out of order and blew it out through the gaping exit wound in his abdomen. Six more sizzling slugs turned another of Qaddafi's desert lice into a paraplegic by powdering his kneecaps. He managed to crawl forward with his comrades and they all recovered their rifles.

Return fire pinned Stonewall to the ground. He exchanged the partially expended magazine for a full one and whipped up rapid fire dirt around the Land Rover in an attempt to flush the quarry. On his left, Bashir's AK burped a brief string of five. A soldier

138

screamed and threw his piece toward Allah. His soul followed a second later when he staggered from behind the cover of the Limey jeep, blood gushing from a wound in his side, into a deadly deluge of 7.62 slugs made in the land of his Marxist masters.

In a wild spasm of fanciful thought, Stonewall reflected that the Soviets might be giving Qaddafi a lot of help but they hadn't done a whole lot for that guy. Slight movement along the blind side of the Land Rover attracted his attention.

A foot came into view near one of the tires. Stonewall took careful aim and gently squeezed the progressive trigger. A single two hundred thirty grain, copper-jacketed bolt of lightning lashed out and pulverized a Libyan ankle. The dumb-shit desert louse uttered a tremulous howl of agony and hobbled into range on his good leg. A stuttered, three-round burst from the Sidewinder cancelled his meal ticket and closed the *shurtah's* pay book on him. Three down. That left only the gibbled up troopie.

Where had the commie crud gotten to? Stonewall raised up and made a short dash forward. The distinctive chatter of a Heckler and Koch assault rifle chased him. The combat-wise soldier for hire dived forward, did a roll and came up grinnng. He'd located the remaining security policeman.

Kalashnikov 7.62mm rounds chewed at the body of the staff car. Stonewall allowed himself a grim smile. Bashir had located the hidden soldier. Stonewall broke out the remaining glas on the far side and worked his way downward. Chunks of body metal flew into the air under the steady, 12000 rpm, nose-to-tail impace of heavy .45 slugs. The car violently rocked on its springs. Over the detonating ordnance Stonewall thought he heard a faint cry of pain. A second later it didn't matter. Scything bullets from Bashir's AK ripped open the gas tank and an instant later more of the same struck sparks from the pavement.

The staff car went up like a huge orange ball from hell.

A swirling tangerine mushroom rose a hundred feet in the air, its top and outer fringes stained squid-ink black. The shrieks of unholy agony from the unlucky Libyan ended when Stonewall emptied his Sidewinder magazine into the wildly convulsing body.

"All right, troops. Let's saddle up and get outta here. We'll take the Land Rover." Stonewall turned away from the carnage without a glance.

Chapter Thirteen

Stonewall elected to skirt around Sebha. The battle at the roadblock had been close enough to the small town to have been heard. Ahead of them lay the long, 280 mile run to Sokna, through the heart of the Black Mountains.

Actually a high, hot, desert plateau, the area got its name from the proliferation of eroded mesas, capped by sheets of basalt. Broken hunks of the lava lie in confusion at the bases of these pinnacles like scattered children's blocks. As the Land Rover sped along it appeared to be traversing a vast, heaving sea. Heat waves, reflected off the black, glass-like rock created an image of rippling water so profound that, added to the motion of the vehicle, gave an illusion of being aboard a tossing, wallowing boat, adrift on a stormy ocean. As the feeling intensified, Stonewall commented on it to Najid.

"It's a good thing I don't get seasick."

Najid smiled. "This is an interesting phenomenon, isn't it? The Black Mountains have to be the strangest natural wonder in a country full of them. We're fortunate to have plenty of water along. Have you noticed how the effect, combined with the heat, increases your thirst?"

"You're right. I keep wanting a drink, even when I don't need it."

"Take all you want. Sokna is a city of wells. We can replenish our supply there."

"Should we turn West at that point?"

"No. This is the only completely paved highway. A bit

longer, but much quicker to get to Tripoli."

Before Stonewall could reply, his teeth clashed together and he bounced high out of his seat when the right front tire of the Land Rover contacted a huge chuckhole. If this was a high-speed, paved highway, he thought ruefully, he'd hate to see the other, more direct route to the north.

Sokna appeared on the horizon four hours later. The village was entirely enclosed by a high adobe brick wall, topped by decorative rows of mud urns. Crenelations commanded the corners and over the main gate, which provided access for the north-south highway. Over this entrance flew the tricolor flag of Libya, its red, black and green horizontal stripes hanging limp in the post-noon calm, obscuring the large white crescent and star in the wider black band. When they rolled through the open portal, Najid spoke to Stonewall again.

"Sokna used to be a stopping place for the slave caravans. They filled their water-skins here and rested their cargo. That's why there are so many wells."

"That's a grim past for any town. How much control has Qaddafi's dictatorship extended over the place?"

"Not as much as he would like. A few soldiers and a new civil administration. If there are *shurtah* agents here no one knows who they are."

A large public well, complete with a modern electric pump and plumbing fixtures, provided for their needs. Najid suggested a meal and the trio went to a small open-air cafe on the north edge of town. Their arms and desert camies made them look military enough to pass without question. Dark glasses masked Stonewall's light eyes and his Cherokee ancestory did for the rest. Once the meal had been served and the waiter withdrew, Bashir told of the trip ahead.

"It is only a short way from here to Hon and from there to Uaddan, maybe seventy kilometers. The roughest part

142

of the trip comes then. Two hundred ninety kilometers from Uaddan to Bugrein on the coast. It used to be a hard-surfaced road," he shrugged expressively. "But the sands provide no base and years of heavy trucks have pulled the tarmac up into ridges. It is a regular—how you say?—washboard."

"Will it slow us down much?" Stonewall wanted to know.

"No. The only way to take a road like that is fast. It jars your teeth a lot but you don't feel the bumps."

"You're driving, Bashir, do it the way you think best."

"Will we stay the night in Bugrein? It is another three hundred twenty-five kilometers along the Litoranea Highway to Tripoli."

"No. I want to be there at the earliest possible time."

"Not many vehicles use the roadway at night. We will look suspicious," Bashir protested.

"We're using a military car, right? In the dark it should be easy to get by."

"What if a patrol stops us?"

Stonewall's thin-lipped smile held a deadly aura. "Then we can deal with them the same way we got the Land Rover."

The Land Rover drove into Tripoli a little before nine that night. Following Stonewall's instructions, Bashir located the shop on the *Sharia Istiklal* operated by Phil Nichols as a cover. A huge, multi-faceted drill bit hung outside the arcaded front to advertise the nature of the business. A seller of oil field tools, even an American, was always welcome in Libya. Fortunately, the establishment remained open, in keeping with local custom. Stonewall told his companions to wait while he entered.

"What can I do for y'all?" a tall, slender man with thick, curly blond locks and halo thatch of golden fur on his bare arms inquired when Stonewall stepped to the counter.

"Are you Phil Nichols?"

"Yep. Tex Nichols at your service. Who might you be?"

"I'm Stonewall."

Nichols registered surprise. "For Christ's sake, man, you're supposed to be out in the desert."

"I got lonely for the bright lights so I decided to come to the big city. What's the hold up on this end? We don't even know where the fuckin' target is."

"Take it easy, Stonewall." Tex Nichols held up one hand, a placating gesture. "Everything's starting to come together. I planned to leave for Mammaudz's camp tomorrow at four. Can things wait that long?"

"Sure. We had a little problem. Somehow Qaddafi's goons know about Polanski and me being in-country. A patrol came to the oasis and we had to waste them all. The Sharif is moving to another place while I came here to let you know."

"Where?"

"Somewhere near the Zeltan oil fields. My guide, Bashir, knows the location."

"More than better, as our Saigon friends used to say. That puts your base camp almost on top of the site."

"Where is it?" Excitement brought a glow to Stonewall's intense gray eyes.

"It took some doing, but I finally bribed the right official. There is a top secret installation that fits the requirements located about fifty miles south-east of Augila and off the highway in the dunes of the Sekima Sandsheet. It's the only one of its kind, so it has to be the bomb factory."

"Good. We have to ditch a Land Rover we appropriated from the *shurtah*. I'll have Bashir pick up another truck or something and we'll meet you here at quarter of four tomorrow afternoon."

"Suits. See y'all then."

Bashir ditched the Land Rover in a narrow, unlighted, arch-braced street of the Old City. By morning it would be stripped bare by the myriad flocks of waifs and abandoned children who made their living working the streets. The weapons were disassembled and hidden in back packs. Bashir led the way to a main thoroughfare and hailed a taxi.

Najid suggested the Grand Hotel, overlooking the harbor, to spend the night. Formal dining would begin soon for Tripolitans and they would have time to refresh themselves before going to dinner. At the hotel, out of deference to Bashir, Stonewall requested three rooms. As a foreigner, Stonewall had to surrender his passport. He had a false document in the name Henry Morgan. He had suggested it to Trojan's man, Swink, remarking that in the capital of pirates, the name seemed appropriate. Bashir departed from the trio on the second floor. Stonewall and Najid had rooms on the third. Inside his accommodations, Stonewall slipped out of his back pack and left a trail of clothes to the bathroom.

Lukewarm water trickled from the truncated shower nozzle. All the same it felt great to the weary soldier for hire. He lathered generously and let the feeble stream slowly wash away sweat, dust and tenseness. At last he reluctantly stepped out, toweled dry and walked, naked, to the bed. He scrounged in the A-frame pack, coming up with fresh clothes and a bottle of White Label.

Stonewall broke the seal and had a long, satisfying pull on the bottle, then opted for a more civilized glass and some ice, which he had brought up from the lobby. He lit a Kent and eagerly sucked the smoke into his lungs. Another sip and he would start dressing.

A knock sounded at the door.

"Who is it?"

"Najid."

In light of that pleasant event, Stonewall opened the

door without bothering to cover himself. The beginnings of an erection began to stir his flaccid penis. Najid slipped through the narrow passage and hungrily eyed Stonewall's bare flesh. She began to unbutton her blouse.

"Islam teaches that it is not proper for a woman to be intimate with a man who has not been circumcized as Allah decrees." An impish smile illuminated her perky oval face. "But I find it exciting!"

Stonewall crossed to the small dressing table. He hefted the bottle of White Label. "Same as the last time?"

"Oh, yes. Before *and* after."

In light far superior to the shadow-filled tent at the oasis, Stonewall found great enjoyment in the lush contours of Najid's firm, healthy young body. She slid out of practical white underpants and stood, arms and legs akimbo to present herself for his inspection. The small, slightly rounded mound of her belly, that arrowed to flaring hips, intrigued him. As did the sparse wisps of silky black pubic hair that only partially covered her swollen muff. The silky pink lips in her cleft opened outward invitingly, glistening wetly. They seemed to call for closer investigation.

Stonewall stepped closer and, with one hand, began a sensuous exploration. In a few desire-filled moments they sprawled on the bed. Najid gasped when Stonewall entered her. Her arms and legs encircled him, heels pressing against his buttocks to force him even deeper. He found one hard nipple and began to massage it with his lips, sucking hungrily as a new-born babe.

"Oh, yes, Stonewall. That's it. That's the way I like it!" Najid cried aloud while his massiveness churned inside her in steady, powerful strokes, in-out, in-out.

When at last their mutual release came in a shuddering, sweating crescendo of climax, they lay quietly for a while. Lips touched lips, throats, shoulders, amid soft murmurs of delight. Finally they pulled apart. Laughing like adventursome teenagers they showered together to remove the residue of their passion. That gave Stonewall another erection. Nijid knelt in the tilted shower stall and let her tongue flirt with the turgid organ that swayed in front of her face. Then she enclosed it in the warm moist cavern of her mouth and swiftly, skillfully brought the writhing, ecstatic American to completion again. Another quick rinse and they stepped out of the bath.

The lovers dried themselves and dressed in post-coital silence. Stonewall poured them another drink, which they quickly downed. Then they hurried to the lobby to meet Bashir. The happy threesome appeared quite at home while they dined al fresco on the terrace.

Back in Stonewall's room, he and Najid undressed each other. His big, toughened hands grew gentle at their task, carefully removing each article, then dwelling on the newly exposed flesh to softly caress and excite. His consumate skill turned Najid into a moaning trembling bundle of amorous fire by the time he lifted her and carried her to the bed.

"Today, you are going to see the sights of Tripoli," Najid announced the next morning. She and Stonewall had awakened at seven and ordered breakfast in the room.

They sat in the ornate Victorian bed, in the regal splendor of the Grand Hotel, eating delicate crescent rolls and soft, spreadable goat cheese, melon and black, sweet coffee. Najid sparkled with that special glow a woman's body takes on after a good loving. Stonewall, feeling equally rejuvenated by their bedroom gymnastics, condescended to agree without protest.

"What's first on the agenda?"

"The Old City, of course. There's the Jama el-Pasha Mosque, the An-Naga Mosque and the *hamman.* Though I can't go in with you at the Turkish bath. The *suks,* the little shops, are the greatest in North Africa. Then we'll come back near the hotel here to the *maidan,*

147

the big square on the harbor, and take Avenue Omar el-Mukhtar to the Municipal Stadium, the Sports Palace and the Fair Grounds. Omar el-Mukhtar is a great Libyan hero. He became a martyr leading the resistance against the Italians, long before World War Two."

"Whoah. That's a heavy schedule. No time out for a drink?"

"Oh, sure. We'll have lunch at the Del Mehari Hotel, that means the racing camel, on Avenue Adrian Pelt. It's really quite elaborate. It was built in the thirties as a weekend pleasure palace for Mussolini's officers. They have a terrific bar there. Then in the afternoon we can take in the museums of Ethnography and Natural History."

"I'd rather take in the bed."

Najid gave him a playful slap. "You think entirely too much about sex. You have fornicating on the brain."

"That's better than having water on the brain or hairy palms."

"Oaf! Don't you appreciate the greatness of the past? Why, they have items in the museums that go back into prehistory. Rock drawings and rare paintings from before the Egyptian dynasties. Also things from Carthage; Punic writing, letters and maps. There's lots of artifacts of Libyan and Arabic origin, of course. They even have some rare, obscure writings in Tefinac, the language of my people. It is so old and long forgotten that even we don't know how to decipher the manuscripts."

"You're really sold on this stuff." Respect colored Stonewall's voice.

"You bet I am. Qaddafi and his bandits can't last forever. Someday we'll have our country back and the contents of the museums will be even more precious to the people of Libya."

"Okay. You win. I'll go get some culture. Meanwhile, Bashir can buy us a nice, safe, unremarkable truck to haul our buns out of here and meet us at Nichols' shop at quarter to four."

"Oh, Stonewall. I love the way you handle things."

"Including you?"

"Especially me. Shall we . . . I mean, do you want to . . . ah . . . before we leave?"

"I want to 'ah,' anytime with you, lovely lady. Glad to oblige." He took her into his arms, feeling the warmth of rekindled passion expanding his groin.

"I managed to acquire us some clever little toys," Tex Nichols announced when Stonewall entered the oil tool supply store on the Sharia Istiklal.

"Oh? Such as?"

"Eight RPG-Twenty-fours. All loaded and ready to go."

"Now that's my kind of birthday present. Have your boy there help Bashir load them on the truck out back in the alley."

Nichols gave terse instructions to his Libyan employee, who started hauling short sections of well casing out to the squat, Fiat step van. Bashir had obtained it at an extortionate price from its former owner, the proprietor of a whorehouse.

"There's also a couple of cases of Russian grenades and ten thousand rounds of ammunition for Kalashnikovs," Nichols went on, exposing his achievements with all the pride of a father at his daughter's debutante ball. "You have no idea how hard I had to pry to break that stuff loose." His glance went beyond Stonewall and out the dingy plateglass window. Nichols stiffened and reached under the counter.

"Uhn-oh. Trouble coming our way."

"What kind?"

149

"*Shurtah,* if I'm not mistaken."

Stonewall looked over his shoulder. Three men, wearing severely cut, Soviet-made suits stood in the street. One of them held up a commanding hand, directing others, unseen, to hurry into position. Ten uniformed paramilitary security policemen, led by a sergeant, jogged into view and took places across the wide esplanade. A light-armored vehicle drew to a stop beside the plainclothes security agents.

"Oh, shit. They've got enough firepower out there to take on a company," Nichols announced gloomily.

"They'll have a hell of a time getting that many people through that little-bitty door. Let's make 'em come to us," Stonewall observed.

"How did they tumble to this operation?" Trojan's man in Libya asked, mentally reviewing his own actions for any possible slip-ups.

Praticality ruled Stonewall's actions. "They did, no matter how. Let's see how many of those commie bastards we can take out before we have to split." He hollered out the back door to Bashir. "How many of those rocket units have you got loaded?"

"Five, *effendi* Stonewall. Also the grenades and ammunition."

"Forget the rest then. There anyone blocking the ends of the alley?"

"Yes. Both ways. Two . . . no, three men ahead and five behind us. But they aren't making any move to close in."

"Okay. You know what to do when the time comes."

Bashir grinned wickedly and reached into the cab for his AK-47. "Yes, *effendi.* I am ready."

"You and Tex's boy will have to provide covering fire while we haul outta here."

"You say when."

Stonewall turned to the others. "Najid, go get in the truck."

"I can fire a gun."

"Then give Bashir help when he opens up."

"Yes, Stonewall." The girl left, looking disappointed.

"Now, let me open up one of those RPG's." Stonewall walked back among the racks of supplies.

"Here come the *shurtah* pigs," Tex Nichols announced.

"Let them get all the way inside."

"Got ya."

Brass bells tinkled on their spring bracket when the door opened. The three *shurtah* agents entered, two parting like the Red Sea to take positions to either side of the front entrance. The remaining secret policeman advanced on the counter.

"Philmore Nichols?" he inquired in harshly accented English.

Tex stood with his right hand draped casually over the cash register, his left remained out of sight under the counter top. "That's me. What can I do for you?"

"I have a warrant for your arrest, and for that of anyone in your store at the time."

"What's the charge?"

"We are not required to reveal that. Taking into consideration that you know only so well, I see no reason not to. You are charged with treasonous acts against the Libyan state and the Revolutionary Command Council. Specifically with a conspiracy to assassinate Colonel Muammar al Qaddafi."

Nichols put on a sad face. "I'm sorry to say that I can't go along with you fellers."

Eyes slitting in sudden tension, the *shurtah* agent darted his hand toward the pistol in his arm pit under the black, pin-stripe Soviet suit. He got as far as his narrow ebony tie when the front of the counter disintegrated.

Twenty-seven pellets of 00-Buck splashed the front of his white shirt with strawberries. Splinters of wood from the blown-out counter turned his stomach into a pincushion. One flyer, a stray ball of lead, entered his left eye. It burst the gristly optic in a shower of black fluid and burned into his brain. He staggered backward, grunting with the effort of remaining upright, spun on one heel and fell face-first to the floor. Before his comrades could react, Stonewall stepped out from between tall wooden storage bin racks.

He had attached the McQueen silencer to his Sidewinder. It coughed softly, politely and one of the *shurtah* thugs hurtled backward through the plate glass window. Shards of glass flew out onto the arcaded sidewalk along with his bleeding body, which oozed red syrup from a trio of .45 sized holes. Stonewall swung at the hips and triggered off another burst.

Surprise and pain warred on the remaining secret policeman's face when the .45 slugs reached his chest a fraction of an instant ahead of the charge in the second barrel of Nichols' 10 gauge, three and one half inch Magnum sawed-off shotgun.

"Oh, fuck. I thought we were going to do this quietly," Stonewall griped while he hoisted his long-snouted piece in explanation. "Then you come up with that cannon."

In the street, the soldiers had unslung their weapons and taken aim. Those in the center, near the armored car knelt and began to spray the building front with hot lead.

"Let's pull back to the van," Stonewall shouted over the explosive din.

Outside, the turret on the LAV began to rotate, bringing the stubby snout of the 57mm gun into line with Nichols' shop.

"*Oh, Chirst!* Look at that!" Nichols cried, frozen in

152

immobility at sight of the ominous black hole and ugly muzzle brake.

"They're gonna shell us," Stonewall acknowledged in a frighteningly calm voice. He let go of the Sidewinder and let it swing free on its sling. "Awh, fuck it!"

Stonewall dived for the floor.

Chapter Fourteen

Before the big gun could fire, Stonewall came up from behind the counter and aimed the tube of a RPG-24 Soviet rocket at the armored car. With a loud whamm the projectile took off. The room filled with smoke and flame.

The missile struck the glacis plate below the snout of the 57mm gun with a loud clank. A fraction of a second later the vehicle bulged at the seams when the ammunition inside went off and the barrel of the cannon pointed drunkenly skyward.

A fire crackled in the shop, ignited by the backblast of the rocket tube. Stonewall and Tex Nichols scrambled to the back door and jumped in the open rear of the step van. Immediately Bashir squealed rubber and the truck sped toward the security men blocking the alley.

From behind came a rattle of rifle fire. The two surviving *shurtah* soldiers sent hurried, unaimed shots at the departing van. Not so, Tex Nichols, who took time to make sure. He dropped one of their attackers with a short burst from a H & K 7.62mm assault rifle. Another loud blast above Stonewall's head brought his eyes up.

Najid stood with legs braced wide apart, blazing away with a Belgian FN/FAL. The Libyan soldier she aimed at suddenly threw away his rifle, as though it were hot, and clutched frantically at his bleeding chest.

It was the last move of his life.

Nichols' Libyan worker had a MAC-10 Ingram poked out the side door, chattering away at the men blockading them in the alley. Chips of stone and plaster flew from walls, propelled by the steady stream of 9mm slugs spitting from the M-10. Considering good sense and survival superior to duty, the security types ducked for cover.

With the motor laboring loudly in second gear, Bashir brought the truck down on them. Boxes and crates grated and splintered in front of the high steel bumper and one *shurtah* thug shrieked in anguish at being dragged along by the assemblage. Omar swung his Ingram at a right angle to their path and blasted another man out of a doorway.

Nine millimeter jacketed bullets pummeled the staggering, falling man until the deadly little submachine gun ran dry. Hastily, Omar changed magazines and sought another target.

Plenty remained for him to pick from when they emerged from the alley into the midst of the reserve force waiting to storm the shop. Bashir quickly turned onto the board avenue fronting the shop. Civilian pedestrians screamed and ran to escape the fusillade set up by both sides. Stonewall got into the action, kneeling in the doorway beside Omar.

Three forty-five slugs chewed a new bellybutton for a fat sergeant, who sprawled in the path of a speeding *shurtah* car. The bulky body caused the driver to lose control of his vehicle.

It flashed through an arched opening in the arcade of the Sharia Istiklal, scraping off paint and door handles, and launched itself through the wide plate glass window of a brass founder's shop. The contents of the ruptured gas tank came into contact with glowing coals, spilled from an ornamental brazier. An orange-red ball of flame woofed into existence and cremated the occupants of the car.

Stonewall squeezed the trigger through to full auto and let the movement of the step van draw a deadly line of .45 holes along a file of soldiers rushing to intercept their vehicle. A soft flutter, like the leathery wings of Death, accompanied the ejection of spent cartridges from the silenced piece. With no recoil, creep or climb, the Sidewinder handled like a jewel. It drew new appreciation from the soldier for hire for its superiority over his former favorite the Uzi. Five desert lice sprawled on the sidewalk before Stonewall had to swap magazines and look for a new threat.

He quickly found it. Wavering flickers of muzzle flame winked at them from a staff car nosed to the curb a few feet from the blazing light armored vehicle. Stonewall hosed it down with quick five-round bursts.

Fat .45 slugs bulled their way through Detroit iron, flattening their blunt noses in the process and slapping into all-too-vulnerable human flesh. A young officer, in the uniform of the security police, thrashed on the rear seat a moment before the upper half of his body flopped through the shattered window.

Hot damn! This is my meat, Stonewall rejoiced as he watched Moscow's latest fair-haired boys tumble into death on all sides. Deadly drum beats sounded when incoming fire ranged on the van. Everyone ducked low and Bashir geared up to high and floorboarded the accelerator.

Rocking wildly, the step van skidded through a right turn off a the *Sharia Istiklal* and hurtled down a narrow side street. A final roar of discharging rounds from Najid and Tex and the battle ground dwindled into distance.

"Close," Tex observed through tight, whitened lips.

"Close, hell," Stonewall shouted back over the racketing of the overburdened engine. "Those dummies were like targets in an arcade shooting gallery. If Qaddafi's whole army is that fucking incompetent, we could take his country away from him."

156

"How do we get out of town?" Najid asked sensibly. "The description of this van will be all over Tripoli by now."

"Good thought, pretty lady," Stonewall acknowledged. He leaned over Bashir's shoulder. "Where can we dump this thing and get new wheels?"

"Already taken care of, *effendi* Stonewall. I suspected we might have difficulty so another truck, a canvas topped Italian-made Fiat awaits us in a small warehouse near the harbor."

"Were you ever a Boy Scout, Bashir?"

"Oh, no, *effendi*. I grew up among the Tuareg. Though I did meet some scouts when I went to school in England."

"Whatever, you're a marvel."

Bashir evaded any attempts at pursuit and pulled the step van to a stop before the wide doors of a warehouse a block from the redolent waters of the harbor. Omar jumped out and opened the overhead and the now notorious vehicle slid inside. Quickly transfer of the supplies Nichols had acquired began. In ten minutes, the Fiat two ton truck rolled out under the lowering overhead door and disappeared into the swelling post-siesta traffic.

"There'll be roadblocks," Nichols reminded the others.

"We'll bluff or shoot our way through," Stonewall announced. "So you were in 'Nam, too."

"Wasn't everybody? Yeah, I got in a couple of tours. I even have my 'Southeast Asian War Games, Second Place' teeshirt."

"What did you do?"

"I was a Sneak and Peek medic."

"I'll be damned."

"Yeah, I know. Wasn't everybody in Special Forces? Hey, I didn't notice any chow," Nichols changed the subject.

"That just proves Bashir is human after all. We'll hit a

157

grocery store in Qasr al Qarahbulli."

Najid winced. "Your Libyan pronunciation leaves a lot to be desired. The name is *KAH-sur al Kaw-ra-BOOli*. And don't expect to find a super market. It's a fishing village we went through in the dark. The best we can expect is some dried fish, figs, dates and melons."

"That beats the hell out of Cee rations," Stonewall observed. "Do you think we could find some scotch? My last bottle got trashed by a stray Libyan bullet."

"No chance. There isn't even a European style hotel in the place."

"Now that's what I call roughing it," Stonewall complained.

"Poor baby," Najid consoled in the same mocking tone he had used.

"There's a police check-point ahead," Bashir interrupted the by-play.

"Let's get ready." Stonewall drew back the cocking knob on the Sidewinder.

Bashir slowed down through the gears and braked to a stop. A uniformed policeman walked smartly to the driver's side of the Fiat and extended a peremptory hand.

"Your papers, please," he commanded.

Immediately Bashir's face became a mobile display of pained confusion. He waggled his hands in hopeless protest. "Always it is the papers," he wailed. "I am a poor date grower from Misurata and know nothing of such things. We have no papers in order to travel in our town. Why must you have this thing? It is a curse that even Almighty Allah could not contend with."

"You must have papers or you will be taken to jail. A, ah, an incident has occurred in the city and all persons trying to leave must be identified."

Stonewall vaulted the tail-gate and dropped soundlessly to the street. Passers-by paid no attention. They had long ago learned the proper etiquette for survival in a

Workers' Paradise. He rounded the rear of the Fiat and raised his Sidewinder.

"*Putt-puttyput!* The submachine gun spoke quietly.

Like five pounds of shit in a two pound bag the policeman hit the pavement. Another hushed, three-round burst shattered the glass in the police kiosk and the other cop's heart.

"Get rolling," Stonewall called to Bashir. He leaped into the rear of the truck while the gears clashed.

A hundred yards off the highway, the Fiat parked in a grove of date palms, five miles east of Qasr al Qarahbulli. The occupants munched on the pinkish-orange flesh of Mediterranean melons, dried fish and sweet, fresh figs. Najid had also managed to procure some loaves of round, flat bread. Stonewall licked melon juice from his fingers and rose to peer out the back of the truck.

Overhead the drone of a single engine reminded them of the manhunt being conducted for the fleeing adventurers. Stonewall had no trouble spotting the light observation plane. It clawed through the sky, following the highway toward Tripoli. They might not find a better time to move on. Perhaps there wouldn't be another aerial search for some while. He went forward and spoke through the open partition between the cab and body.

"We ought to be moving out. That spotter won't be back this way until he's covered all the ground from here to Tripoli."

"Yes, *effendi.*" Bashir put aside a salt-encrusted fillet of halibut and started the motor. The plane had flown out of sight by the time the Fiat reached the highway.

Stonewall's small party reached Baugrein two hours before sunset. A short airstrip on the southern edge of the town gave Stonewall an idea.

"It will take the rest of tonight and most of tomorrow to get where we're going on the road," he told the others. "And on the ground we're vulnerable. There's an Aero Commander over there that can haul the load we've got and five people easily. It can get us there, cross-country in a little over an hour and a half."

"How do we convince the pilot to take us?" Tex inquired.

"I can fly it," Stonewall informed him. "We'll simply steal it."

Bashir drove the Fiat truck up to the small office building attached to one side of a long, corrugated iron sheeted hangar. The door was locked and no one seemed to be around the airfield. Quickly they approached the high-winged, twin engine Aero Commander and began loading the cargo aboard. Stonewall reviewed the pre-flight check list, installed in a small scroll case atop the instrument panel.

"Bashir, can you handle the right hand seat?"

"Of a surety, *effendi*. There is nothing with a gasoline engine that I can't drive or fly."

"Good. Let's get this thing pre-flighted, fire it up and haul ass."

Twelve minutes later, Stonewall slid the fuel mixture levers to full rich, shoved the throttles forward, kicked on the carburetor boost pumps and released the toe brakes. The Aero Commander lumbered down the macadam runway and lifted gracefully into the air. An hour and forty-five minutes later, with ample daylight left to make a landing, Bashir spotted Achmed Mammuadz's Tuareg camp in the desert south of Augila. He pointed excitedly, jerking one of Stonewall's sleeves to get his attention.

Stonewall nodded and used smoke from a cooking fire to verify wind direction. He banked sharply dropped the flaps and lined up for a quick touchdown.

Five minutes after that he cut the master switch and accepted a bottle of White Label from Hank Polanski.

"Does the guy who owns this thing know you borrowed it?" Polanski inquired.

"He does by now." Stonewall went directly to the Sharif's tent.

"Good news, *effendi* Stonewall," Achmed greeted him. "My chief scout has located the bomb factory."

"That's great. I brought Tex Nichols along, so we can verify the site." Stonewall unrolled a map he had carried and pointed to a spot in the Sekima Sandsheet.

"Hummm. That is not where Abu Bakr claims to have found the installation. It is here, on the other side of the highway about fifty miles north of Tazerbo."

"Oh?" Stonewall walked to the flap and called outside. "Tex, you want to come in here?" When the lanky Texan entered the tent, Stonewall showed him the map. "Achmed's scout says that the Libyan bomb factory is here, not in the Sandsheet."

"My source was entirely reliable."

"And I trust Abu Bakr implicitly. If he says it is here, then that is where it is."

"The thing to do is take a look," Stonewall suggested. "Besides we need to recon it before the attack."

"Yes, that does make sense, *effendi* Stonewall," the Sharif agreed. "When do you wish to make the reconnaisance?"

"Tonight. We'll leave here at midnight."

A Coleman lantern cast a bright glare in Stonewall's tent. He sat with Polanski, going over the plan for the recon and sipping from a bottle of White Label with a significantly lowered content.

"Ain't that a kick in the ass. Now we got two places this bomb factory is supposed to be. How much faith do you put in this Abu Bakr, Cap'n?"

Stonewall didn't get to answer. A disturbance at the outside resolved into Ms. Melissa Gould. She stood in the entrance in trembling, white-lipped fury. "I hear you murdered a whole lot more innocent people, you fascist bastard."

Stonewall ignored her. "What is she doing on the loose?"

"She behaved herself on the trip over here so the Sharif ordered her released, provided she stay in the confines of camp."

"Horseshit."

"Goddamn you! I asked you a question."

"Did you? I thought it was another of your bullshit propaganda statements."

"One day we'll rid the world of all you right-wing reactionary dinosaurs," Melissa railed. "Oh, wait, just wait until I tell the real story of what's happening here in Libya."

"Crap. You're so full of Marxist fantasies that you couldn't tell *real* if it kicked you in the ass. As a general rule, I never kill anyone who isn't trying to kill me first. In your case, I might make an exception."

Overwhelmed by rage and self-righteous indignation over the account of Stonewall's battle in Tripoli and his escape, Melissa could only resort to epithetical cliches. "Assassin! Murdering lackey of the CIA! Running dog imperialist!"

An agitated Bashir appeared in the entrance behind the girl. Stonewall nodded toward Melissa. "Get her out of here. And this time see that she stays bound and gagged except at feeding time."

"What's the matter?" Anger turned to taunting. "Is a cretin like you incapable of answering an intelligent argument? Or are you afraid of debating a liberated woman?"

"You know, you remind me a lot of Karol, *Ms.* Gould."

"Who's she? The sister you no doubt sleep with?"

Stonewall let the insult slide by. "No. She's a liberated liberal lady lawyer I know back in Fayetteville. Whenever she gets off on one of these asinine tantrums I just fuck her until her eyes cross. That usually drives the idiotic liberal garbage out of her head." Stonewall started to rise, forcing a lustful look on his face. "I might try the same cure on you."

"Rape! A rapist and a baby-killer. It fits. The typical Amerikan soldier."

"You have such a low opinion of all of us, why don't you move to Mother Russia? Or are you aware that they don't think too highly of loud-mouthed troublemakers in their own country? Out! Get her out of here!"

Bashir grabbed Melissa's shoulder. She shook him off and started to reply. The look of black, implacable anger on Stonewall's face changed her mind.

A high chain-link fence, topped by loops of ribboned concertina wire, lay bathed by floodlights atop tall poles at each corner. At intervals along it, bright yellow placards warned everyone to stay clear in Arabic and Italian. On each was the international symbol for radiation. Something about it seemed out of kilter to Stonewall.

How did they propose to keep their nasty activities secret if they advertised so openly? He studied the squat, sharp-edged concrete buildings behind the wire. No windows. They could house anything, including booster pumps for the oil transmission pipeline. Guards with attack dogs patroled inside the fence. In the distance he could hear the whine of a jeep motor, indicating an outside roving sentry.

"What do you think?" he whispered to Polanski, who lay beside him in the sand.

"You could tell me it's Qaddafi's royal shithouse and I wouldn't know the difference. What does an atomic bomb factory look like?"

Suddenly the jeep engine roared louder and the buff, gray and pale green camouflaged vehicle bounded over the dune upon which they lay. Bright light bathed them.

Salim, one of the trusted squad leaders, reared up and blasted out the headlights. Stonewall took out the windshield and the top of the driver's head. A big, 14.5mm Soviet machinegun, mounted on a crossbar behind the front seats, began to puke bullets at them.

Stonewall and Salim threw grenades at the same moment. The twin blasts disintegrated the jeep and its passengers.

A siren wailed to life inside the compound and spotlights began to criss-cross the desert outside. Two machineguns, located in tall towers, came alive and began to stitch sand and lizards. More of the security force poured from one building and the big front gate swung open.

"Let's get outta here," Stonewall called to the other members of the small recon patrol. They ran to where a young Tuareg held their horses. Two more jeeps roared into the desert.

Stonewall kicked his mount in the ribs and took the lead. Behind him, strung out like ghostly pearls on a cheap necklace, came Polanski and four Tuaregs. Bright headlamps washed over them as a jeep crested the dune in a cloud of sand and raced toward the fleeing figures. Stonewall raised his left arm in a signal and the horsemen split into two groups of three, headed at right angles from the path of the oncoming jeep.

Before the driver could compensate for this new tactic, Stonewall, Salim and Muktir whipped their horses into a lathered frenzy and streaked down toward the jeep. Bright red muzzle blooms opened up the night. Slugs clanked into metal and two punctured the right front tire. Bouncing and jolting in the back, the machinegunner tried to swing the Soviet-made

14.5mm toward the attacking force. He worked in vain.

Stonewall concentrated his Sidewinder's fire on the dark bulk of the standing soldier. A long rip of .45 caliber slugs splashed into the receiver of the KVP heavy and sent a shower of sparks into the operator's face. The stinging metal bits arrived a fraction of a second behind three two-hundred thirty grain, lead-filled copper jackets. Blood squirted from the machinegunner's ears and distracted the driver, who fought the deflating tire.

Without warning, the jeep fell off to the right, reared and flipped over. No one survived.

Stonewall and his patrol wheeled their steeds and galloped off toward the security of the rolling dunes.

Chapter Fifteen

"Looks like your contact in the Defense Ministry wasn't all that trustworthy, Tex," Stonewall remarked to the Libyan contact man. "They had enough stuff out there to hold off a battle group."

"There was supposed to be tanks. Did you see any tanks?"

"No. Not any indication of there ever being any. Of course, if one piece of information was false . . ."

"What do you plan now?"

"Practice for the assault here in camp, get what rest we can and move out about midnight. We will attack at dawn. I'd like to get a daylight look at the place. With that firefight last night, that's out. We'll have to wing it."

"We could take the airplane," Tex suggested.

"That would advertise our intentions even better than our Ms. Gould. Speaking of Gould, I want her to go along. It might do her some good to see what this is all about."

Polanski took a deep swallow of *tibra,* belched loudly and shook his head in disgust. "I still think that's a mistake. Hell, Cap'n, first chance she gets, she'll let out a yell that'll draw those desert lice right in on us."

"Not if she's gagged. Bring her here," Stonewall decided. "Let's see if she's ready to talk sense now."

Polanski and Bashir returned with the American reporter. Her hair had gone lank, lost its earlier luster and springy quality. She had stubbornly refused to change clothes and her safari outfit had become creased and dirt-encrusted, with several large food stains prominent on her blouse. Stonewall's nose wrinkled when she entered the tent.

"Ask Najid if some of the women can bathe her and get her into fresh clothes. The Libyans could smell her approaching from down wind."

"I understood this was supposed to be some sort of conciliatory meeting. I might have known better."

"Ms. Gould, I don't want to be offensive. Your own attitude has created this situation and it is necessary to get you cleaned up, whether you feel insulted by it or not. Once you're cleaned up, I'm more than willing to talk with you, provided you will be objective about it."

"Your chauvinism is showing, Lawrence," Melissa Gould flared, referring to the *kafeyah* and *agal* Stonewall had been wearing since returning from Tripoli.

"Call it what you like, I feel it is important for you to know what is going on."

When Melissa had been taken away, Polanski brought up another subject. "Why haven't they sent out any patrols after that contact last night?"

"Could be they considered it a raid by bandits or a demonstration of anti-government feeling by Tuareg tribesmen. There were only six of us, on horseback. Not exactly a major threat to a security chief."

"I hope you're right. Me, I think Tex here has the right of it."

"We'll see soon enough, won't we, old buddy?"

When Melissa Gould returned, looking surly, though considerably more fragrant, Stonewall offered her a steaming cup of mint tea. He reminded himself to control his temper.

"That's much better. I enjoy looking at attractive women. Not just the physical attributes, but because I appreciate beauty. Let me guess. You must have learned those cute tactics from some student activist group. Let yourself go, look as dirty and bedraggled as

167

possible so it can be blamed on pig brutality and mistreatment, right?"

"I was in the SDS," Melissa admitted between sips of the sweet, strong-flavored tea.

"It figures. Now, Ms. Gould, we are going to destroy the atomic bomb factory tomorrow. I want you to go along so you can see the truth. What I don't want you doing is making any noise, yelling to warn the enemy."

"The *enemy*," Melissa's full, tempting lips turned down in disdain. "Is that how you see everyone who isn't a flag-waving zealot like yourself? Patriotism, Mr. Stonewall, is the last refuge of scoundrels."

Stonewall sighed. "I thought you understood that this conversation was to be free of your trite Marxist shibboleths."

Startled by Stonewall's vocabulary, Melissa leaned forward. Curiosity roused, her reporter's instincts took over. "You sound like an educated man, Mr. Stonewall. Whatever could possibly have made you . . . what you are?"

"Meaning that I should be an enlightened liberal? Well, I suppose I was, about a lot of things at least. What changed me? Some of your communist heroes, Ms. Gould. The Pathet Lao. They took a young school teacher, a girl not unlike yourself, raped her and ripped out her guts. We were going to be married." After a tensely crackling silence, Stonewall went on.

"After that I had a different outlook. They were no longer merely citizens of a different country, trying to do what was right by their lights. They were fucking animals! And the goddamned barbarians who made them that way, the Russians and Red Chinese, were even more responsible. I didn't stay safe at home in some dingy back-streets apartment labeled, 'revolutionary headquarters,' and watch neatly sanitized strips of film made in Hanoi. I went out and saw for myself. Now, that's what runs me. What about yourself, Ms. Gould?"

Melissa swallowed a surprising lump in her throat. "I . . . I'm sorry about your girl, Stonewall."

"No, no, you're not really *sorry*. The sorrow is all mine and it can't be shared." He drew a deep breath. "How about it? Will you agree to keep quiet, and objective, and find out what the hell is really going on out there?"

"Do I have any choice?" Melissa hurried on, in the face of Stonewall's scowl. "I don't mean that to be flip or sarcastic. I mean it sincerely, I *must* know the truth. I'm opposed to nuclear arms, like any reasoning person. If what you say is true, then I have to see it, photograph it and tell the world."

"Thank you, Melissa." The words came out almost a sigh.

Melissa seemed unaware of the use of her first name. "I'll not cause you any danger. Trust me."

At 0015 hours, the forty man attack force moved out from Sharif Mammaudz's encampment. Fully armed, their training complete and tuned to a fine pitch, they felt cocky and confident. Even Stonewall accepted success without any misgiving.

Twenty minutes before dawn, the strike force reached positions outside the compound. The single, roving patrol had been neutralized by Salim's squad without a shot being fired. When the platoon of desert fighters had been dispersed around the target, Polanski reported to Stonewall.

"Don't it seem a little funny that there aren't more guards outside the fence? You'd think they'd maintain at least a low level alert after last night."

"Different strokes," Stonewall whispered. He began to sweep the compound with powerful night glasses.

Objects stood out clearly in the bright floodlights that turned the area inside the fence to daylight. On

169

one pass, a door opened. Stonewall froze, watching carefully. A man stood in the doorway, back partly turned toward Stonewall, talking to someone inside. The squat, thick-shouldered figure turned fully into the light.

"Pete Guterrez," Stonewall spoke aloud. A sardonic smile creased his cheeks. They had come to the right place. He turned to Bashir. "Bring Ms. Gould along once we've secured the gate and get inside."

"Yes, *effendi.*"

A red signal flare rose into the coming dawn.

Assegai in his left hand, the Sidewinder humming a deadly tune in three note bars, Stonewall charged down on the fence with the rest. Ahead of him the gate guards fell, bodies convulsing and gouting blood. A barrack door flew open and armed Libyan soldiers spilled out. They tumbled in the hail of flying lead. Stonewall made it to the gate and saw a Tuareg blast apart the chain and lock that secured it, with a short burst from an AK-47. Leading the others, he rushed inside. He looked around for his main target, Pete Guterrez.

Guterrez had disappeared.

Stonewall pressed on. He waved with the assegai for his section to follow. A short dash carried them to the building where the soldier for hire had seen Pete Guterrez standing in the doorway. More Libyans appeared. Crossfire from the Tuaregs hammered them to the ground. Stonewall found the door barred against him.

A brief burst from the Sidewinder weakened the portal. Before Stonewall could kick it in, a grenade blasted near-by.

Steel slivers slashed the air around the crouching soldier of fortune. He felt a piece slam into the aluminum tubing of his A-frame pack. In front of him, the door violently shuddered and drunkenly swung inward on one hinge until it grounded against the concrete floor.

A wall of zipping projectiles shrieked out over Stonewall's hunched form. He jerked a grenade from his pack harness, pulled the pin, slipped the spoon and counted a quick two before he threw it into the room.

Smoke, concrete chips and dust blasted out the doorway in a halo of flame, followed by the screams of the dying and wounded. Stonewall dived through the opening and came up spraying the room with .45 slugs.

When he remained the only living human, he made a quick check of the corpses. Again Guterrez had escaped him. He headed for an inner door, blown from its hinges by the grenade.

Beyond it lay another room. In it, Pete Guterrez.

The renegade American worked to bind a field dressing around a slight shrapnel wound high on his left arm. A sneer distorted his lips and his face contorted with anger.

"You sonofabitch, Stonewall."

"Why did you throw in with these assholes, Pete? Never mind that. Where are the bombs?"

Guterrez laughed. "You fell for it, sucker! This ain't the place you're lookin' for. It's a trap, you stupid *gringo cabrón!* You're all gonna die."

Stonewall swung up the muzzle of his Sidewinder.

"Hey, man, I ain't armed!" Guterrez pleaded. One hand groped behind him and closed over the solid bulk of a field telephone. With all his strength, he hurled it at Stonewall, striking the white-haired soldier of fortune squarely in the chest.

Stonewall released his hold on the submachine gun and staggered back. Guterrez launched himself at his opponent, a sharp-edged machete in his right fist.

A quick move by the assegai blocked Guterrez's first slash. The two men jumped apart, probing, testing. Stonewall flicked the tip of his weapon forward. Sparks sprang from the point of impact when Guterrez countered. He looped the machete down and under with a swipe for Stonewall's chest.

Stonewall dropped the point of his assegai and a shock ran up his arm when the opposing steel smashed against it, edge to edge. When they broke apart, Stonewall noted a deep notch in Guterrez's blade. Stonewall let his arm droop and took a deceptive half-step backward.

Guterrez immediately lunged. In the next instant he realized his mistake. His lips formed a desperate, pleading NO!" though the sound never left his mouth.

Cold Zulu steel slid between the sixth and seventh ribs on his right side. Exquisite pain flooded Pete Guterrez's body. Fire, curiously covered with an outer layer of cold, blossomed in his right lung, which rapidly began to flood with his own blood. He recoiled in reflex action, which jerked the broad, leaf-shaped blade of the assegai from his chest. His machete clattered to the floor, dropped by nerveless fingers. His vision turned swimmy and his knees bent at odd angles. With a small moan, Guterrez collapsed. Stonewall knelt at his side.

"Where is *Noor Mawt*. Pete? Where? C'mon, you bastard, it's not your problem. Where is Project Death Light?"

"Sucked you in good. Y-yer all gonna die. Won't do ya no good. Th-the real place is th-thirty klicks north, on the other side of the road." Guterrez vomited up a huge gout of blood, trembled until seized by a state of rigidity a moment before he died. Stonewall cleaned his assegai blade on the dead man's shirt, stood and checked his Sidewinder.

"You deceived me! You bastard you lied about the whole thing!" An ashen-faced Melissa Gould stood in the entrance, one hand grasping the door jamb to keep from swaying. Revulsion and horror made her features ugly.

"We were all taken in. And I know who is responsible."

"No! No! You came here to k-kill him. I saw it all, heard. You *are* a CIA assassin. That was an American you killed because he worked for Libya. Murderer!" she shrieked.

Stonewall crossed the room in three long strides. He caught the edge of Melissa's screaming mouth with a hard backhand blow. Shocked out of her hysteria, Melissa began to sob.

"Listen to me. If you want to get out of here alive you have to do exactly what I tell you. Get your shit together and stick close. This was a trap. The real bomb factory is thirty kilometers north of here. If we don't get away quickly we'll all die. Do you understand?"

Melissa nodded woodenly and shrank back when Stonewall reached for her shoulder. Fuck it, he thought. He brushed past the shaken girl and headed for the outside.

Two hundred Libyan soldiers poured from concealed bunkers and rushed toward the small invading force. Three Tuaregs went down in a mist of flying blood and sand. Stonewall methodically killed four of the five Libyans who had blasted them. From the corner of his eye he saw Melissa Gould emerge from the building and follow him. He made a short dash to a burning truck between them and the gate. Fighting desperately against enormous odds, the Tuaregs fell back. Stonewall cut loose a final burst.

Damn, the last of his .45 ammo. He came to his feet and raced for the yawning gate. Melissa struggled behind.

Outside, he quickly rounded up three men to serve as messengers and checked his radio. "Striker One, this is Striker."

"Go ahead, Striker, I got you," Polanski's voice came from the tiny speaker."

"What's your situation?"

"Beside desperate? We'll make it out of the compound, Cap'n."

"Good. Make your move now. I'm organizing a rear guard. Striker out." Stonewall turned to Bashir who had materialized at his elbow.

"Take care of Melissa. Go with the main force and help Polanski where you can. I'm taking the rear guard."

"You should not, *effendi*. We need you for later on."

"I fucked this up, I'm gonna make sure your people get out with the lowest losses possible. Now move out!" Stonewall growled.

"Yes, *effendi*." Bashir took the unresisting Melissa by one arm.

"Salim! Over here," Stonewall yelled over the continuous crackle of small arms. "Form up a reinforced squad. Two rocket launchers. We'll fall back slowly to the vehicles and haul ass."

"Yes, Captain. Stop! Take cover here," he shouted at the demoralized raiders streaming past. "Behind this dune. Return their fire, you blind she-camel!"

Stonewall had breathing space to examine their situation. In-coming fire had begun to slacken. The reason made the problem worse. Most of the Libyan soldiers busily boarded trucks and half-tracks, preparing to run down the invaders. Slowing down that pursuit had to be the first order of business.

When the first gunner with a RPG-24 showed up, Stonewall pointed down the long sand slope to where a half-track filled the main gateway. The rocketeer needed no words to tell him what to do.

A freight-train roar and a thin smokey trail connected the light rocket tube with the steel-sided vehicle. A tiny puff appeared at a spot immediately behind the cab.

In an eye-blink, huge flames leaped skyward, bearing along chunks of men, damaged weapons and sheet metal. A thick column of black smoke, laced with bright orange flickers, engulfed the armored troop carrier and, when the ammo let go, the gas tank ripped open, adding more fury to the blast. Men screamed and slapped at flames that played over their uniforms and flesh while they made a vain attempt to escape their immolation.

"That'll hole 'em a while," Stonewall observed. "Let's pull back."

Behind the next line of dunes the rear guard took time to set up. Some of the Libyan troops remained afoot and would be after them regardless of the obstruction at the gate. Stonewall carefully checked fields of fire and ammunition supplies. Then he waited.

A line of helmets came into sight first. Along the distant ridge, twenty Libyan soldiers appeared, moving with caution, arms at the ready.

"Not now. Not now," Stonewall urged in a hoarse whisper. "Let them get closer. Much closer."

On came the desert lice, encouraged by no sign of the enemy. Downhill momentum brought them to a trot by the time they reached the facing slope. Still Stonewall cautioned his men to wait. The Libyans advanced.

Six of Qaddafi's finest came within grenade range.

"Now!" Stonewall bellowed.

Three of the Tuaregs hurled spherical Russian fraggers. The security police died before they could react. AK-47 fire poured down on the rest of the searchers. Five more bodies jerked, twisted, fell. The remainder threw grenades of their own and rushed forward.

Beyond the ridge they found the sands empty except for expended casings. The elusive foe had disappeared. Steeled by their experience, the survivors started out with added caution, tracking by scuff marks in the sand. One bold Libyan took the lead to the top of the next dune.

He had the honor of being first to spot Stonewall's read guard. He died shouting that intelligence when a

.45 slug from Stonewall's 1911A1 Colt zipped through his open mouth and punched a circular flap from the back of his head. He splashed his comrades with brains, fluid and blood.

A dozen Kalashnikovs rattled their deadly chorus and once again, Stonewall ordered a withdrawal. Another dune to climb and they would reach the jeeps. Adversity had sharpened the tactical sense of the sergeant leading the Libyans. He refrained from immediate advance and sent five men around his right flank in an attempt to infilade the quarry. He also sent a runner back to the compound to notify his captain that his men had kept the raider force in contact.

That delay allowed Stonewall and the rear guard to make their way to the two jeeps and an ancient, dilapidated Ford truck. The men quickly loaded aboard. Stonewall checked them out and headed for the lead vehicle.

A hot pain exploded in the flesh under Stonewall's left arm with the stunning impact of an iron fist. Nearly on top of the fierce stab, came the sound of a shot. Stonewall staggered and caromed off the rear of the jeep. He went to one knee in the same moment that Salim swung up his AK and built dust columns out of sand.

Uttering a faint cry, a Libyan soldier reared up, then collapsed onto the near side of the dune. His body rolled toward the rear guard, small blotches of blood making circular tracks. Stonewall hauled himself upright and slid into the jeep. Four more rifles opened up from the ridge. Return rounds grew in volume from the Tuaregs and one prudent desert warrior fired a rifle grenade.

The finned oblong exploded two feet above the ridge. Groans and a gagging, retching sound rose from the opposite side. Salim slapped the driver on his shoulder and the lead jeep, with Stonewall hanging on in the back seat, shot forward. A final burst came from the lumbering

Ford truck and then the three vehicles crested a rise and dropped out of sight.

"They'll have that gate clear by now," Stonewall shouted over the motor noise to Salim. "We'll have a dozen vehicles on our ass."

"Some of the Muktar Tuaregs took the liberty of obtaining a few land mines. It would be wise if we returned off the road."

"What about aircraft?"

"Not before we reach safety."

Satisfied for the moment, Stonewall began to struggle with the harness straps. "Help me get out of this so I can take a look at the wound."

"You are hurt badly?"

"I hurt like hell but I don't think it's serious. I can move my arm freely. Got to stop the bleeding."

"Yes, Captain." Salim climbed in the back and applied himself to exposing Stonewall's left side.

A curtain of blood washed down from a pair of neat holes, the entrance wound puckered and bluish-lipped, the exit point an angry red. Stonewall sighed with relief when Salim told him it could not have passed through more than an inch of tissue. The grizzled soldier for hire scrounged in a map pocket and produced a bottle of White Label. At least he had a little pain killer for the trip to camp.

Chapter Sixteen

"Where is Abu Bakr Hamza?" J. C. Stonewall yelled in fury when the rear guard at last returned to the camp.

"Did he not go with you on the raid?" Sharif Mammaudz inquired.

"Yes. And the main body has been back a long time. Where is he?"

"He did not return. Perhaps he fell in battle," the Tuareg leader shrugged.

Mollified for the moment, Stonewall answered quietly. "That could be. If he's alive, though, I'm going to hunt him down and blow him in the weeds. We walked into a trap. He helped set us up."

"You're going to get that wound treated first," Phil Nichols advised. "If you don't, you won't be doing much of anything."

"Hell, it's only a scratch."

"I saw scratches like that turn into amputations in 'Nam."

Reluctantly Stonewall walked to the former medic's tent. He grudgingly permitted Nichols to remove his fatigue jacket and the field dressing. Tex handed him a bottle of Johnnie Walker and Stonewall took a long swallow. By the light of two Coleman lanterns, Tex probed the wound.

"You're lucky. A clean wound and I couldn't seem to snag any fragments of cloth. I'll stuff it full of this gooey yellow gunk and bind it and you should be good as new in a couple of weeks."

"Only if I get to keep your Black Label. You've got good taste in scotch."

"Thanks."

Polanski appeared in the open tent flap. "Hey, Tex, I promoted up a little poker game. You in?"

"Later, maybe. I have to finish up on Stonewall."

"Oh, hi, Cap'n. I heard you took a light one."

"And rushed right out to find me. You're all heart, Hank."

Polanski looked embarrassed. "I got a full report from Salim the minute you got back. Besides, we're about to wind this thing down and I'm ahead by what I calculate to be five gallons of *tibra*. I want to make sure I have enough to make it back to Egypt and good, cold beer."

"Hopeless case," Stonewall told Tex Nichols.

When Nichols finished his ministrations, Stonewall walked through the cool night toward the tent where Melissa Gould had been confined. Starlight, and occasional glowing braziers of charcoal, lit his way. The moon had already set. The soldier of fortune felt a vague dissatisfaction with himself. Why did he feel required to make some sort of explanation to this liberal female reporter? On the abortive raid she had seen only what she wanted to see. Yet, the compulsion rose strongly in him to make another attempt to reconcile reality with her pre-conceived notions. He paused at the entrance-way, uncertain how to proceed.

"May I come in?"

"How can I stop you?" Melissa snapped.

Stonewall entered. The delicious odor of crisply roasted goat and earthy smelling *cous-cous* reminded him that he had not eaten all day. The long, perilous journey back from the false bomb factory had not allowed for any pauses. He had chewed some strips of dried goat and drank water to replace the loss of fluids. Now his stomach growled in protest while he watched Melissa consume large quantities of the food arrayed on a low, inlaid table in front of her. Utilitarian, brass, oil-burning lamps provided the only illumination. Intricately woven wall-hangings of pastoral desert scenes covered the black hide walls. The soft light somehow made Melissa appear vulnerable. Stonewall cleared his throat, though she spoke first.

"They told me you had come back. I can't say that I shed tears of joy over it."

His resolve to be patient and seek a means of giving understanding disappeared. "You were supposed to remain objective about the purpose of the raid. It's obvious that you are incapable of objectivity."

"You're a fine one to talk about that!" Anger flared in her sparkling eyes. "What was it you called that American you murdered? A *fucking* commie, a traitor! Who gave you the right to decide what side is the best, what way of life is suited for the peoples of this world? Two-thirds of the world's population now live under one or another form of Marxism. They seem to find it satisfactory. It's only a few red-neck reactionaries like you who insist on fighting the tide of history."

"What a crock of shit!" A vision of holding Melissa close to his chest, consoling her and explaining away her misgivings fled from Stonewall's mind. In two seconds their conversation had degenerated into another shouting match.

By eleven-thirty Stonewall had a considerable buzz on from the scotch he had consumed. A small, shy boy scratched at the entrance to his tent. When the soldier for hire looked up and motioned for the youngster to enter, he did so, taking short, pigeon-toed steps. He extended a grubby hand, nail-bitten fingers holding a slip of white paper. Stonewall took it and the kid fled, giggling.

Najid had written the short message. It asked him to come to her tent. Stonewall rose, unsteadily, located his boots and slid his tired feet into them, but didn't bother to button his shirt.

A single oil lamp lighted the interior of Najid's quarters. She lay on a huge pile of pillows. Stonewall felt an eager warmth radiate from his loins when he looked at her. She wore a brief, diaphanous costume that tantalizingly revealed the lush contours of her bronze-olive body. With one graceful arm she gestured toward a low, onyx and lapis lazuli inlaid table. On it sat a bottle of White Label.

"I found us . . ."

"I brought a . . ." Stonewall hefted his own bottle.

They laughed together.

"At least we will have plenty of scotch," Najid observed when their humor subsided. "Same as before?"

"Yeah." Stonewall removed his shirt and undid the buckle of his trousers. "Before *and* after."

Najid didn't bother to snuff out the lamp.

Overhead, the great constellations, dramatic in their clarity in the inky desert sky, had wheeled across the heavens. Stonewall's Rolex read four-thirty. Relaxed and content, his loins drained, the soldier of fortune walked through the quiet camp, savoring the goodness of being alive. Najid. Jesus, what a woman. Born in one of the few truly primitive societies left in the world, she had been educated in England and France. She saw herself as liberated by Tuareg standards, though soft and compliant in bed. She could give a eunuch a hard-on.

Between their energetic bouts of lovemaking his bottle of scotch had been emptied. He carried only his boots in one hand and the Sidewinder in the other. The sand felt good under his bare feet. Thoughts of Najid continued to fill his mind until he reached the closed flap of his tent.

A sudden, furtive movement between two goat-hide dwellings caught his eye. Abu Bakr Hamza stepped out of the shadows.

"So, you escaped the trap we had laid for you," he said in broken English. He didn't see the submachine-gun slung over Stonewall's shoulder. In his right hand he held a Makarov 9mm automatic. Its muzzle end sported a fat, ugly silencer. Abu Bakr uttered a short, impatient grunt.

"That leaves me the task of liquidating you. It will end my usefulness here, destroy my cover. A small inconvenience, compared with the necessity of eliminating you before you find the real facility." Abu Bakr brought the Makarov into line with Stonewall's chest.

With a swift movement, Stonewall dropped to his left, right hand clawing at the pistol grip of the Sidewinder. Abu Bakr's Russian pistol coughed once.

The bullet cracked past Stonewall's ear.

Then he had the sweet little SMG tightly in his grasp. He swung the muzzle-heavy, silenced piece under his armpit and squeezed through to full auto even as the weapon came into position on his forearm.

A spray of 9mm slugs burned into Abu Bakr's crotch, slapped their way upward, making a figure-eight of his navel before chewing up coils of intestine, pulping his liver and shattering his sternum. Stonewall had converted the little chatter-gun to 9mm on his return from the raid and had no lack of ammunition. More of the copper-jacketed hornets stung Abu Bakr's throat and face.

He jerked and cavorted, driven backward until he tripped over a guywire and crashed to the earth. Abu Bakr Hamza convulsed mightily and died.

"Now I have you! Defiler of our women! Blasphemer of Allah's chosen land!" Ali Hammad al Taliq screamed in Tuareg. A billowing burnoose swirled around him when he charged out of the darkness further down the street, brandishing a large, curved *yatagan*. The wickedly sharp scimitar whistled through the air. In his dervish frenzy, Ali Hammad seemed unaware that Stonewall had blasted Abu Bakr into doll rags with a silenced submachine gun. He wildly swung the blade, aimed at Stonewall's exposed neck.

Quickly Stonewall raised the Sidewinder. Violent impact sent a shock up his arm. Ali Hammad's sword had cut nearly half way through the cannister of the silencer. Well, that's fucked, Stonewall thought clinically. He gave a powerful yank that sent Ali Hammad stumbling off balance and freed the Sidewinder from the kiss of steel.

Ali Hammad recovered and began to leap and dart about. Stonewall had no time to remove the tube of the suppressor and in its damaged condition it would probably spit slugs in a dozen directions. Aiming would be futile. He daren't fire indiscriminately. The chance of wounding or killing innocent Tuareg women and children was too high. He made his decision quickly and darted into the tent.

"Coward! Come back!" Ali Hammad shieked.

Stonewall returned in a second, clutching his assegai.

Tensely, the two men faced each other. Ali Hammad began to stamp, twirl and chant. His eyes rolled up in his head and Stonewall sensed his opportunity. He lunged forward, the tip of the assegai leading the way.

Swift as the deadly desert asp, Ali Hammad struck downward. The well-honed edge of his *yatagan* missed Stonewall's hand by a fraction of an inch. Stonewall drove his left fist into the side of Ali Hammad's head. It seemed not to bother him.

"*Che succede?*" Stonewall yelled in Italian.

"I'll tell you what's going on," Ali Hammad responded in the same language. I'm going to kill you."

"*Per che cosa?*"

"You are an American and you must die. You killed Abu Bakr Hamza, who had promised to help me. For that you will also die."

"Abu Hamza was an agent of the *shurtah.*"

Ali Hammad slashed with his sword again. "That is true. He told me so tonight when he came back to camp. What did that matter to me? I would gladly have taken aid from the evil *djin* themselves if it helped killed just one American."

"What has that to do with it?" Stonewall blocked another thrust, sought an opening.

Black rage congested in Ali Hammad's face. "My father was an American! He abandoned us, my mother and I. To survive, I became a boy whore. It . . . it left me impotent. I can not enjoy a woman. And it . . ." The *yatagan* flashed again and Stonewall felt a burning line drawn across his shoulder, dangerously close to his neck. ". . . is all his . . ." Metal screeched on metal. Stonewall barely managed to parry the blow in time. Pain jangled through the wound in his right shoulder. The attack left Ali Hammad wide open. ". . . fault!"

Stonewall drove the assegai forward with all the force of his shoulder behind it. Ali Hammad's cry of psychological anguish turned into a bleat of mind-numbing agony. The tip of the Zulu blade slid between two rows of whitely flashing teeth, pierced the brain pan and scrambled cerebral tissue before bursting out the top of Ali Hammad's head.

In a sudden silence, Ali Hammad's mouth worked like a fish out of water. His lips seemed to caress the blade that distorted them. His body went rigid and he rose on tip-toe. Stonewall gave the assegai a vicious twist and pulled it out. The blade made an ugly, sucking sound.

Ali Hammad fell on his face in the sand. Blood

poured from his ravaged mouth and skull, forming a pool around his head. Stonewall looked up to see Sharif Achmed Mammaudz standing near-by, silently watching everything.

"You knew about his past?" Stonewall panted.

"Yes. When he first came to us, he told me of it. I felt sorry for him. Perhaps now he will sleep in peace."

"He will sure as hell sleep." Sudden exhaustion washed over Stonewall. He felt weak and vulnerable. "I must get some rest," he made his excuse to the Sharif. "Tomorrow the camp will have to be moved and we must plan for the attack on the bomb factory."

"Good night, Stonewall. May Allah bring you peace."

"Here it is." Stonewall and Polanski sat with the squad leaders of their strike force in the back of a large truck while it rumbled across the desert sands. Their destination was the shelter of another oasis not far from the compound where Qaddafi's minions built atomic bombs.

"Look closely at the layout of the buildings. This is the diagram Tex Nichols brought along. See the distance between the outer fence and these low structures? There is a possibility it is mined, though informants say it isn't."

"We will attack according to plan," Polanski took up the briefing. "Ramad, Baktir, your squads will be with me. We will go in here. . ." Polanski pointed to a symbol on the map. "Where the spur line from the railroad passes through a gate in the back. We'll want covering fire from along this ridge. One rocket launcher and three AK's. When the interior guard is secured and no more resistance on the surface, the fire team will move in also."

"What about tanks?" Salim inquired.

"There are supposed to be some. At least three. They have to be taken out first or there'll be blood, guts and feathers all over the place," Stonewall informed them. "Also keep a lookout for jeep patrols and air cover. After all that has happened the Libyans will be antsy as hell."

"How long will we have inside?" Ramad queried.

"Not more than an hour. Maybe less. That's from the first shot fired until we get through underground."

"Under . . . we will beneath the land?" Ill at ease, a new replacement picked to take Abu Bakr's position as scout, asked.

"We'll be there, not you. You and the drivers will have to hold the surface until we come up. Then disperse according to how we rehearsed it earlier.

"The men with Polanski," he went on with a new subject, "will be responsible to locate any stockpile of bombs and damage them beyond use. Then mine the whole area. When it blows, there's gonna be one hell of a lot of dirty desert. All effectives must be at least five miles from the bunkers, with a lot of sand dunes between you and it, when the blast goes off. Once you booby-trap the atomic bombs, link up with my section, wherever we are, so the job can be finished and we can get out."

"We attack at first light tomorrow?" Salim inquired, his face mobile with eagerness, eyes alight.

"Right. Like the last time. Only this one's for real."

Chapter Seventeen

Darkness cloaked the approach to the bomb factory compound. Three trucks and four jeeps comprised the small column containing the strike force.

During the afternoon, after the cavalcade of the Tuareg band had made it unobserved to the small oasis of Q'dahm, two small patrols went out to locate rapid transportation. They came back with three oil company rigs, wide-tired, high-center trucks specially built for desert use and far superior to the rattle-trap Ford used on the previous raid. Salim's squad also managed to ambush and capture two Libyan army jeeps, complete with 14.5mm Soviet machineguns. The big .52 calibers would add considerable firepower to the assault force and would be used to cover the rush on the road and railroad gates. Stonewall contemplated his preparations with satisfaction and reflected on his last meeting with Najid . . .

She brought him a bottle of scotch an hour before the evening meal. "Cocktail time."

They toasted each other with a suddenly somber reticence. "You won't be coming back," she observed simply.

"No. If this works, Polanski and I will be pulling out for Egypt."

"If you fail?"

"I won't be going anywhere. Here or Egypt."

"And Col. Qaddafi will have his nest of American spies to show off to the world." Najid's voice turned bitter, "With ample assistance from that communist-loving bitch reporter, no doubt."

"Not likely, this time."

"Why?"

"I've decided to see that she dies before I do."

"Lord, you're a hard man, Stonewall."

"In or out of bed?" His suggestive words and vibrant closeness broke the mood.

"In bed, oh, yes. Let's see how hard you can keep it in bed this time." She began to unbutton his shirt . . .

A sudden, persistent swelling between his legs interrupted Stonewall's recollection. He glanced at his Rolex oyster. In ten minutes they would be hitting the bomb factory.

Fully a hundred floodlights projected a glowing penumbra into the pre-dawn sky over the atomic bomb factory complex. Suddenly the elements winked out to glowing spots of orange. A soldier's combat-honed instincts clamored at J.C. Stonewall that this moment of sight-destroying blackness had to be the right time. He keyed the talk switch on his AN/PRC-6.

"Open fire." So calmly did he speak the words he might have been wishing someone good afternoon.

Lambent trails of green Soviet tracers laced the compound, seeking and finding targets in the brief confusion of the extinguished lamps. The stream of 14.5mm slugs at the front gate found a tall guard tower and disintegrated it in a shower of wood and glass. Men screamed, feeble sounds against the cacophony of hell from the yoke-mounted machineguns. Suddenly a yellow-orange blossom illuminated the muzzle break and squat turret of a Soviet T-55 tank.

A shrieking shell roared over the gun-mounted jeep at the front gate, fifty yards from where Stonewall orchestrated the attack. Already fat packages of explosive whizzed on courses toward the two visible armored monsters.

Before the Soviet-trained, Libyan gunner could slide another brass casing into the breech, an RPG-24 rocket struck thin metal plate below him. The shaped charge detonated and hurled globules of molten steel and hot gasses through the tank's side. Sprays of the liquid metal showered into the ammunition compartment.

Even while a shriek of mindless terror rose in the gunner's throat, the racked shells exploded.

The tank's sides bulged, flame gouted from hatches wrenched off their hinges and out the splintered barrel of the main gun. Turned into a fifteen ton frisby by the confined blast, the turret took flight, wobbling across the compound to crash thunderously into a concrete barracks building.

A fraction of a second later the second T-55 acted in a similar manner. The sailing turret left behind the lower halves of the tank commander, gunner and loader, to be cooked into crispy critters in the roiling inferno from fire-belching diesel fuel compartments. Stonewall keyed the radio again.

"All right, move out."

"Ul-ul-ul-ulululul, Allah Akbahr!" In the grainy light of pale dawn a dark wave of Tuaregs swept down the sloping dunes toward the beseiged compound. Tiny winking flashes identified the AK's they fired in disciplined bursts of three and five rounds. What magnificent fighters they made, with so little training. Stonewall raced along with the first assault wave, his spirit buoyed by the thought.

With two thousand men like these and six months to train them, he could take all of North Africa back from the fucking Reds!

Slightly ahead of Stonewall the main gate splintered open under a smashing blow from the second jeep on his side of the compound. In the rear seat, the occupants blasted with their Kalashnikovs and hurled grenades at sand-bagged machinegun emplacements. Stonewall charged through behind the little vehicle and squirted two survivors.

Nine millimeter slugs crumpled this last resistance and a quick spurt of speed brought the soldier for hire to the sidewall of the barracks assaulted by the tank turret. He heard the moans of injured inside, gauged which room and hurled in a grenade. The grenade cracked and silence followed. This was the life!

And oh, God, how he loved it!

Stonewall breathed deeply of the pungent odor of powder smoke and blood, drew his assegai left-handed and made a short rush to another building. From the other side he heard the pugnacious growl of another T-55 diesel engine. A moment later the ugly snout of the 100mm smooth-bore main gun poked beyond the corner. Control motors whined in the turret and the long barrel rotated toward the railroad gate, which stood open, presenting its deadly fire at the Tuaregs who rushed into the complex.

Beyond the tank, which opened withering, accurate fire on the hapless invaders from its three machineguns and the main snorter, Stonewall saw fleeting movement. The figure of a man darting from the cover of low structure to another. Polanski!

In one hand he carried a squarish satchel charge of RDX. Where the hell were the rocket launchers? Stonewall glanced to his left, where Bashir hovered under cover, close to him, as though attached by a string.

"Bashir! Bring me a satchel charge." The young Tuareg jumped at Stonewall's command.

"Here, *effendi*. I have already inserted the detonator."

"Good." Stonewall set the charge for a five second delay on the time pencil. "We're gonna kick shit outta that tank."

Bashir grinned. "It will be an honor for me."

"I'm going to do it. You cover me."

Bashir looked crestfallen. "Yes, *effendi*."

Stonewall waited until he saw Polanski dash toward the hulking side of the huge Soviet tank, then pushed the actuating plunger and ran forward with light, springy steps. The old friends met over hot Russian metal. Stonewall slid his canvas bag of death under the belly pan, the most vulnerable spot on the behemoth. Polanski positioned his satchel charge under the lip of the rear glacis.

"Scram, Cap'n. This turkey's gonna blow."

Three seconds later an enormous blast shook the building. The T-55 cracked in half vertically, squeezed by incredible force. The concussion, in the confined space of the T-55's innards squashed the crew like over-ripe tomatoes. Polanski scuttled forward again and dropped two white phosphorous grenades down a sprung hatch.

Billows of white smoke rose in the air. Stonewall motioned Bashir to bring Melissa Gould forward and held a hurried, squatting conference with Polanski.

"Hank, take your people to that low structure over there. It's supposed to be the entrance to underground storage and warehousing facilities. Locate those fucking bombs and rig them for the blast. Take her along."

Melissa looked at Stonewall, eyes wide with fear and excitement. "God, this is big," she blurted out, stripped of her usual leftist cynicism. Stonewall ignored her. "Those are Russian tanks. One of them shot at me."

"Kill anybody who moves down there, but make sure all charges are set before you cross through the tunnels to where we'll be." He pointed to the building they had scrunched down beside.

"Bashir, you and Omar will be in charge up here.

Set up a defensive strong point around each entrance. Waste anyone on the surface and hold on until we come up. Oh, yeah, one other thing.

"Polanski, see that Miss Marxist America here gets plenty of pictures. Keep her camera clicking." Firing stopped and an eerie silence held over the smoke-and-dust shrouded compound. "We'll move out in two minutes."

"Check," Polanski acknowledged.

"You say the word, big fellah," John Wayne answered from Bashir's lips.

"Oh, Christ, *oh, Christ!* I'm surrounded by madmen," Melissa mumbled. Polanski grabbed her by one wrist and dragged her toward the distant building.

When the two minutes passed, Polanski turned the crank on a small hand detonator. The small diamond-packs of C-4, connected by primacord, went off with a loud crack. The hinges shattered and a large, thick metal door crashed out of its casement. Two Tuaregs rushed forward at Polanski's signal before the smoke drifted away. They hurled two fraggers and a white phosphorous grenade inside.

In the next instant following the blast Polanski led the way inside. The sturdy M-14 in his hands blazed at the shadowy figures of the survivors who sought to flee the onslaught. One Libyan, in the uniform of a security policeman, threw up his arms, pirouetted gracefully enough to put Nureyev to shame, then plopped with undignified akwardness across a splintered desk.

In the other building, Stonewall ran into instant resistance. A dozen Libyan soldiers barricaded the main hallway and fought with grim determination. Mixed among them, six men whose white lab smocks and broad Slavic faces marked them as Soviet technicians, fired at the invaders with a mixture of weapons.

Two Tuaregs went down with barely audible groans before three grenades rebounded from the walls with loud cracks. They landed to either side of the barricade and detonated with a shattering roar. Parts of bodies, plaster, blood and slivers of steel flew through the air. Stonewall leaped from a smashed doorway and ran forward.

He drew his assegai and drove it into the fat gut of a moon-faced Soviet slob who tried to blast him with a Stechkin 9mm machine pistol. The Zulu terminator ripped through thick layers of yellow-white fat and spilled purplish coils of quivering intestine onto the floor, already slick with Russian blood.

"Die, you Ruski mother-fucker!" Stonewall shouted. His wild laughter echoed off the walls. This was more like it! The heart of all his dreams. Killing pig-fucking Russians. He could do this all day without even a coffee break.

Another technician, who had a gushing head wound from a grazing piece of shrapnel, gazed in bug-eyed horror while Stonewall disemboweled his comrade. He saw the fires of near-madness in the eyes of the blood-lusting soldier of fortune and raised trembling hands to ward off doom.

"*Nyet! Nyet!* Please, no," he repeated in English.

"*Da!*" Stonewall bellowed in his quaking face. "When you get to hell, you Russian bastard, tell Karl Marx I think he's a stupid fuck." Stonewall swung the assegai.

A meaty smack accompanied the African blade through the Soviet technician's neck. His head flew from his shoulders and rolled down the hall. His scalp wound stopped bleeding.

A final rush down a narrow, unlighted corridor brought Polanski and five Tuaregs to a large door. An electronic combination lock, a box attached to the wall with ten toggle switches protruding from its top, controlled egress. Polanski had a simple answer.

"Bring me that flat-faced Russian technician," he ordered.

When two Tuaregs came forward, with the small, frightened scientist, Polanski growled at him. "Do you speak English?" The Russian nodded. "Good. Now, are you going to work that lock for us?" He shoved the muzzle of his M-14 into the Soviet's crotch. "Or do I blow your balls off?"

Quickly the Russian technician manipulated switches. There followed a moment of buzzing and clacking, followed by a loud, metallic click. The captive reached out and gave the door a shove. Excellently balanced, despite its weight and thickness, it easily swung on its hinges.

Inside bright lights illuminated a long table, fitted with a rack made up of a dozen padded cradles. In six of them rested highly polished, cylindrical metal objects that resembled plumb bobs. The walls were covered with thick slabs of dull gray lead shielding. On a small stand near the door a geiger counter clicked in a slow, deliberate rhythm. Polanski motioned for Melissa Gould to be brought forward.

"Welcome to your basic nuclear arsenal," he commented dryly.

"Are those things for real?" she gasped.

"A lot more real than I'd like 'em to be." He turned to the Tuaregs and Phil Nichols, spoke in Arabic. "All right, you know what to do. Get started on the main charges and let's see what we can do with the bombs."

From down the hallway came a brief rattle of gunfire. Melissa began to take photographs of the bombs and the room. In a few minutes three strike force members entered, bringing with them four Libyan technicians in soiled lab smocks. The prisoners looked

194

like death warmed over. Small patches of hair were missing from their usually thick, oily black locks. One evidenced large, running sores and all four had a faint rash, like a speckled blush, that discolored their faces.

"My God, look at them, that's awful," Melissa commented to Phil Nichols.

"Radiation sickness," Tex observed. "Apparently Qaddafi didn't have the money or the time to provide proper safety measures. Or maybe he didn't give a damn. You oughtta get pictures of them, ma'am."

Polanski hustled the Libyans forward. "Here's what you're gonna do for us, fellahs. You're gonna open the inspection plates to the controls on those bombs. Then you cut the wires to most of the shaped charge. That way the sphere is gonna blow on only one side."

"Won't that expose them to dangerous radiation?" Melissa protested.

"What difference does it make? They're dead already. It'll only speed up the process. Besides, they're the sons of bitches who helped build these things. *Isri'*, *Isri'!* Hurry up," he shouted to the Libyans.

Under threat of the guns, the technicians began to do as ordered. Melissa took a full roll of film, walked out into the corridor to change and returned, shutter clicking.

"Those poor men," she commented to Polanski. "I can't believe an enlightened man like Col. Qaddafi would allow something like this to happen."

"You'd better believe it. That Ruski we got to open the door has a touch of radiation poisoning, too. If we don't get out of here soon, we'll be lucky if any of us ever has kids."

"What do you mean? It is safe, isn't it?"

"Come here, I'll show you." Polanski led Melissa to the geiger counter. "See this? It's been set on an extremely high range. Let me set it on the grid for normal radiation." Polanski turned a dial and the regular, metronomic ticking became a wild flamenco of staccato clicks.

Melissa paled. "You mean we're gonna wind up like, like them?"

"It's still in what's called normal range," Polanski assured her. "That don't mean a hell of a lot. Who knows the future effects that might develop? These turkeys have been around high level emissions for weeks. They've had it. Excuse me. I gotta go send some boys to plant charges in the stair well."

"It is ready," one technician called in a trembling voice.

Phil Nichols edged forward and peered over the shoulder of one Libyan while he inserted a long-nosed pair of side-cutters into the bowels of an atomic bomb. One misstep at this point, Trojan's agent knew, could turn the entire area into a radio-active crater, them included. The Libyan lab tech clenched his jaw muscles and squeezed on the cutters.

Snick! A crisp, metallic sound came from inside the nuclear device. Quickly he cut through three more wires. With a sigh of relief, he moved to the next bomb.

Stonewall's section had reached the lower level of the huge bunker, where the laboratories and assembly area were located. They had met little resistance on the upper floor, where living quarters for the scientists and recreation rooms opened off the tee-shaped passageways. The instant they reached the first lab, they found out why.

A cataclysm of hot lead screamed out of the open doorway, copper jackets screeching a banshee wail as they distorted on concrete walls. The deafening sound of almost continuous detonations made communica-

196

tion impossible. Stonewall edged forward and peered through the blue haze of cordite-scented smoke. From this vantage point, behind the corpses of two Tuaregs who had fallen one on top of the other, he made a quick evaluation.

Pop! The striker fell and a handgrenade sizzled and fumed in Stonewall's hand. He lobbed it overhand into the lab. Right behind the blast he led the way into the chaos of broken retorts, mangled stands and splintered counter tops. Salim, Rashid and three others followed.

Three Libyans reared up, rifles roaring in the confined room. Stonewall cut them down with his smoking Sidewinder. A stream of 9mm slugs from a MAT-49 slammed into a lab bench an inch above the soldier of fortune's head. The tall, ugly desert louse who held the cheaply-made French piece didn't have time to correct his aim.

Two out of three 9mm pellets from the Sidewinder destroyed the ball joint of his right shoulder a fraction of an instant before 7.62 slugs from Salim's AK-47 ripped out his throat. Stonewall waved casual acknowledgement and the attackers moved on to the next room.

Boris Zmeyá and the remaining Russian technicians, six of them, crouched behind an improvised fort of boxes, crates and heavy steel desks. The KGB Captain could not believe the amount of destruction wrought by a single man, leading so few troops. Dark forms appeared in the doorway and Zmeyá jerked the extension stock-holster of his Stechkin machine pistol to his shoulder. A stream of 9mm bullets chewed up concrete and the metal door frame. He cursed bitterly. At least two men had gotten inside the room.

Stonewall heard the familiar yammer of the Stechkin and zeroed in on its location. Fire poured in on him from three directions. The soldier for hire ducked low, then yelped when a stray round struck the heel of his boot. His clothing tugged at his body when holes appeared in the loose sides of his camie jacket. Stonewall saw movement near where the Stechkin had fired and cut loose a long burst.

Gurgling around a fountain of blood, a white-coated technician rose to his feet, staggered a hesitant step and pitched into eternity, his body draped over the barricade. In the distance, two solid blasts jarred the underground complex.

Good. That meant Polanski and his men had completed placing charges in the storeroom and had sealed all the entrances to the area. A momentary chill washed over him. What if there had been a big radiation spill in the process? What the hell, he didn't plan on having kids anyway. Stonewall frowned at the buzzing slugs that kept pestering him. He drew out a small, pale blue-green spheroid, with a yellow band around its bulbous middle. He pulled the pin and flipped the white phosphorous grenade over the barricade.

A soft plop sent smoke-trailing bits of the burning white metal and billowing clouds toward the ceiling. Amid shrieks of agony two Russians leaped over the barrier, clawing at the hideous bits of chemical that ate into their flesh. They ran toward Stonewall, crying in their native language that they wanted to surrender.

The Stechkin snarled in a soprano register and the technicians pitched forward, dead before their faces ground into the cement floor. A flash of insight told Stonewall that, true to cold-blooded Soviet logic, the KGB man assigned to shepherd these scientific sheep had terminated them to prevent witnesses getting into undesirable hands. He swung the Sidewinder toward the enclosure and trashed a file cabinet between him and the KGB man. A sudden commotion drew his attention to the yawning entrance to an unlighted tunnel.

Dust and smoke billowed out, followed by Polanski and his men. Stonewall began to inch his way up over a heavy piece of equipment. Sparks and crackling noises issued from its interior. It led Stonewall to conclude he had climbed on top of the atomic facility's computer. From his vantage point he could see a cluster of three men in line to ambush Polanski and four Tuaregs, who stalked down a corridor between tall banks of electronic cabinets. He could not bring direct fire from where he lay. A quick look around gave Stonewall an idea.

Overhead he spotted a manually operated chain hoist on a gantry rail. Stonewall tucked the hook into his left armpit and held on tightly. He kicked off with both feet and went sailing across the room. From above he rained down streams of hot slugs that chopped into the huddled Libyans. He quickly twisted his body and stopped his advance with a solid rappel off the far wall. Something tickled the back of his consciousness.

He had not drawn fire from the KGB man. Had the phosphorous finished the agent off? Below him the volume of battle increased to a crescendo. Powder smoke blended with that from small fires and destroyed equipment. Confusion ruled the scene for thirty long seconds.

Then came utter silence.

Stonewall lowered himself to the floor. A quick check of the scattered corpses told him that Tolliver and Byrd were not among the dead. Inspection of other rooms on the bottom level also failed to produce the turncoats. Stonewall consulted with Polanski.

"I saw three guys duck through a narrow door over there just before you took off on that Tarzan act." He pointed toward an opening to the left of the pile of furniture.

Stonewall checked his watch. "The numbers are

gobbling at our ass. We have to make sure those pricks bought it. You get the explosives set while I make a check. Give me five minutes, then set the timers and let's get out of here." He strode to the door, that opened onto a small alcove which gave access to an elevator. Stonewall punched the call button. Nothing happened. Jammed open somewhere. He started for the stairs.

On the surface again, Stonewall discovered the bodies of Omar, Tex Nichols' Libyan assistant, and three Tuaregs. No sign of Bashir. One of the jeeps was missing.

Shit, Stonewall thought. Now we have to go after the bastards.

Chapter Eighteen

Quickly the wounded were loaded aboard the trucks, then joined by the remaining Tuaregs. The plan called for Achmed Mammaudz's tribe to split up for a period of three months before gathering once more at al Hamdillah. Stonewall and Polanski, Tex Nichols and Melissa took one of the machinegun mounted jeeps. Stonewall included an unfired RPG-24 with the other supplies. At the last minute, with the seconds ticking off toward a huge blast that would saturate the area for several miles around with deadly radiation, Bashir rushed up.

"*Effendi*, it would be better were I to come along. There is always need of an extra gun."

Stonewall made no effort to veto the offer. "Are the others completely aware of how important it is to get clear of this area by at least five miles?"

"Yes, *effendi*."

"And they will stay down between the dunes?"

"Yes, *effendi*."

"All right, let's roll."

With five passengers the jeep struggled to overcome the overload. Rated as a quarter-ton truck, the weight of the ammunition for the 14.5mm KPV machinegun exceeded that of two persons, the small vehicle had exceeded its listed capabilities. The engine labored to pull such mass up and over the shifting dunes of the sandsheet. They made seven miles when the ground violently shifted under the wheels.

Immediately the rolling timpani beat of staged explosions reached them, muffled by coming from underground. The geiger couter, which Polanski had prudently brought along from the storage vault, began to clatter a warning. Bashir speeded up.

"There goes Qaddafi's big chance," Stonewall commented.

No one answered. Melissa sat in the rear, beside Tex Nichols. Her face had gone slack, eyes looking at some distant horror. Subdued and pensive, she swayed with the movement of the jeep and licked dry lips. Shallow tracks in the sand, from a single vehicle, told Stonewall they had come the right way.

"The highway." Bashir braked and pointed down a long, undulating slope. Far in the distance, a tiny dot could be seen hurtling through the heatwaves.

"They'll be headed for Benghazi," Tex stated.

"How can you be sure?" Stonewall wanted to know.

"It's the only large city close at hand. That KGB agent you told me about will want to contact his consulate and the other two will want to get the hell out now that the project has been demolished."

"I'll buy that. Bashir, how fast can you make it to Benghazi?"

"Nearly five hundred kilometers?" The young Taureg hesitated. "Five hours, if we are lucky. There is a governor on the engine and we have an overload." He looked meaningfully at Melissa Gould.

"Make it in four and I'll take you to the states with us."

"I can disconnect the govenor in ten minutes time."

"Do it," Stonewall decided.

This couldn't be happening. Marc Tolliver's mind refused to accept such easy, overwhelming defeat. Only four of them left? He and Byrd, Mustafa al Hawaadi and that KGB prick, Zyemá. Shit, the guy's name meant *snake*. Could probably be trusted like one, too. Fucking J. C. Stonewall! One man couldn't do it. He had been one of the best, Tolliver reminded himself. So had Stonewall.

Even so, he and the two ex-Special Forces men he'd recruited for Qaddafi's bomb project had trained the security forces until they squeaked with efficiency. Nothing like this should have happened. A cold, sick feeling nearly bent him double. He'd worked so *hard*.

Everything lay in ruin. All his plans to carve out a little empire of his own, an oil rich one, which he could rule any way he wanted and have both East and West bowing and scraping to cater to his wishes. God, it all seemed so real only yesterday.

Then Stonewall came along. Lousy fucking mercenary! Stonewall had wasted Pete Guterrez at the decoy site, that much had come through before the radios went out. Then he'd come on like the Rams line at the factory itself. Men died by the bushel, stumbling over each other like the Keystone Kops. Bunch of fucking parade ground soldiers. They'd retained nothing of what he had tried to instill in them from his vast combat experience. Stonewall and a handful of Tuaregs. Now, that's who he should have gone to with his plan. But then Qaddafi would never have backed him.

Qaddafi! Oh, shit, that fucking ego-maniac would want a large chunk of Marc Tolliver in order to save face. He'd better figure out some way to get out.

"Mustafa, until things cool off, it might be better if I got out of the country. Can I get a flight to Rome from Benghazi?"

"It would be wise if you remained available to Col. Qaddafi. He may have . . . questions." Al Hawaadi let his thin lips slide into a nasty, insinuating smile.

"I understand. We can work out the details later. Have you had any luck with that radio?"

"Yes. An entire battalion is being mobilized. Also air cover will be called in within the hour. None of those responsible for this catastrophe will escape." Mustafa looked hard at Marc Tolliver. "None."

"Choppers, Cap'n." Polanski's words brought Stonewall back from a dark reflection in which he trod the dark jungles of Southeast Asia once more.

"The hunters have found us. Stop here, Bashir."

"But *effendi* . . ." Stonewall's scowl ended his protest.

"Those birds can fly faster than we can drive. They're easy to shoot out of the sky, though."

When the jeep came to a stop, the helicopters had closed to about two hundred meters. Stonewall stepped onto the macadam roadway. He held Polanski's M-14 in his hands. One finger touched the fire selector and turned it to full auto.

"Sittin' ducks," Polanski murmured while he swung the long, cooling jacket-covered barrel of the KPV toward the further chopper.

An ear-punishing roar erupted from the 14.5mm machinegun. Smoking tracers, their green light barely visible in the bright, mid-morning sun, arched toward the helicopter. Tiny specks appeared to fly from the metal body. The craft staggered in the air, lurched and began to fall, the main rotor in autorotation. A wisp of smoke spurted from the engine compartment an instant before the entire craft became enveloped in a huge orange ball of flame. Polanski started to shift his aim to the remaining craft, saw he had no need to and rested his arms over the hot receiver of the KPG.

Stonewall had taken aim at the nearer machine. The plexiglass windows of the cockpit starred and splintered under steady assault from the 7.63mm rifle. A line of holes walked back and up toward the air intake for the jet engine. Chunks of metal wouldn't do the turbine blades any good. Pin-pricks of light flickered in the open waist door. Sand flew from the verge near Stonewall's right boot. He changed magazines and fired another burst.

A loud cracking noise came from the engine. The main shaft stopped turning and the loud thumping sound of the rotors ceased. One long, wide blade snapped off. The chopper tilted to one side and hurtled to the earth.

It landed with a tremendous impact and burst into flame.

"We've got a jeep to catch," Stonewall commented when he climbed back into his seat.

"There'll be more," Polanski advised.

"How's your ammo?"

"We're about a hundred pounds lighter and there's two big boxes left. I make that a thousand rounds."

An hour sped by without any noticeable increase in speed, though the speedometer needle indicated seventy. It began to appear that they had driven beyond the search area. The first indication that they had not outrun their troubles came when a freight train streaked over their heads.

A huge hole blasted into the tarmac fifty yards behind them. Then Stonewall saw the threat.

Tank!

A giant T-10 from the squatty, truncated-pear silhouette of its thick-armored turret, that loomed over a small dune near a curve in the road three hundred meters ahead. The huge 122mm main gun snorted again. The projectile burst on the opposite side of the road, less than thirty-five feet behind the jeep. Bashir fought to control the careening vehicle. Another round and they'd be right on target, Stonewall estimated.

"Hand me that RPG-24," he shouted over his shoulder.

Tex Nichols complied, checking first to see it was properly armed. Stonewall gave the rocket tube a quick once over. Only seconds remained before they got blown into eternity. The big gun in that fifty-five ton behemoth could fire three rounds a minute. The third one wouldn't miss. Then the utter desperation of their situation struck him.

Where could he use the rocket? Its shape charge would not penetrate the enormous glacis of the turret. What the hell, though. Anything would be better than simply waiting to die. Then the tank commander made a fatal tactical error.

Anxious to eliminate this enemy, whom his head-quarters informed him, had been responsible for the deaths of hundreds of Libyan soldiers, the young sergeant in charge of the T-10 ordered his driver to pull out into the roadway. The Christie carriage groaned in protest and the threads bit into sand.

At first sight of forward motion, Stonewall grabbed Bashir's knee. "Hit the brakes!"

The jeep sloughed to a stop and Stonewall jumped out. He knelt and fitted his eye to the sight. A quick adjustment and he fired.

In the T-10, the driver had applied the left brake lever and the huge metal monster slowly pivoted to line up with the approaching vehicle. Too late!

Riding in the thrust of its solid propellant, the Soviet missile flashed between the left treads and contacted the vulnerable sidebody of the T-10. In an instant the interior turned into a flaming Hell of burning metal globules.

"Wait until she blows, then drive around it," Stonewall instructed Bashir. He tossed aside the useless launch tube and got back in the jeep. Too bad he didn't have more ammo.

Bashir made up for lost time. Ten miles outside

Benghazi, they came in sight of the jeep carrying Tolliver and Byrd. While Stonewall watched helplessly the small vehicle stopped alongside the road and a figure got out. He went to a black Zim sedan and ducked into the back seat. The Russian auto sped away.

No time to chase down that Russian bastard, Stonewall regretfully acknowledged. His job was to terminate Tolliver and Byrd. "Keep after the jeep," he ordered Bashir.

Stonewall reviewed the dossier on Marc Tolliver. He was supposed to have a wife and three children somewhere. Ex-wife, he corrected himself. She had divorced Tolliver when the exposé on the club racket came out. His oldest child, a boy of eleven, would be aware enough to understand how his father had died. How would it effect the kid?

That wasn't his problem, Stonewall dismissed. First he had to frag the turncoat bastard, then it would be up to Mommy to make explanations. Tolliver had been a brilliant company grade officer, although his frequent praise of communist guerrilla leaders and terrorists had been reported more than once. Security checks had turned up nothing derogatory. When he made field grade, Tolliver appeared to have taken on a Messianic complex. A common enough failing. George Armstrong Custer had been a classic example. By all reports, Tolliver had been a good husband and father. He seemed to worship his kids, particularly the older boy and his daughter. Somehow the flaw in his nature had been nurtured and allowed to blossom. No, Tolliver was easy to figure. Howard Byrd, Barry the Bird, however, presented an enigma.

An orphan, Howard Byrd had been adopted by a deeply religious family. Christian Scientists, the army records indicated. That made it odd that he had volunteered for the army at all, odder still that he had not exercised his conscientious objector status to secure a non-combatant assignment. He had no doubt been a snitch since childhood, carrying stories to his parents, teachers, anyone who would listen to his tales. Such children often turned out to be liars and sneaks as adults. When they could not find scandal to repeat, they frequently invented it. The Howard Byrds of the world were generally loners. No one was spared their vicious tongues and consequently they made few friends, and none who proved lasting. That much was easy to see on the surface. What followed tended to seem bizarre.

Byrd must have been radicalized at an early age, in high school and during two years of college. Somehow security investigations had repeatedly missed this fact. A shrink might speculate that this was an extension of his personality. After all, totalitarian societies relied heavily on informers. Stonewall dismissed the theory. It only meant that Barry the Bird was a fucking communist. He had a pretty red-headed wife and two children, and his job with the CIA.

When his employer discovered his involvement with radical leftist causes he had been threatened with dismissal and worse. Barry had taken a lot of photographs of Viet Cong atrocities, committed against innocent, pro-government Vietnamese. They had been used to "document" one of Hanoi Jane's most scathing denunciations of Vietnam war criminals; by which she meant American soldiers. Trojan had developed private information that indicated Byrd's activities had been uncovered much earlier by a loyal Special Forces officer.

Byrd framed the man for the murder of his wife. He had taken the pregnant young woman out in the hills, bound helpless in a sleeping bag and shot her in the head with a .22 Magnum, High Standard derringer that belonged to her husband. Rather than face the consequences of his acts, Barry the Bird had fled to Libya. That pretty well summed up Howard Byrd, Stonewall thought. A liar and snitch, a cowardly asshole who did well enough killing helpless women but didn't have balls enough to face a man. A rattle of small arms fire jerked Stonewall out of his reverie.

Benghazi had been left behind and they faced a police roadblock. From the effort the security troops made to blast their jeep it was obvious they had been tipped off by the fleeing trio ahead of them.

Polanski manned the big Russian machinegun. Three inch long, steel jacketed slugs half an inch in diameter, lashed into the Libyans and lifted them off the ground. Stonewall opened up with his Sidewinder and dropped two more. Melissa covered her face with her hands and screamed. Tex Nichols' Ingram chattered from the left side of the vehicle until the jeep rammed the front fender of a Land Rover and they scraped through the roadblock.

"Close," Stonewall commented.

"Too damned close," Polanski grunted. "I caught one in the ass." He loosened his belt and dropped his trousers. "Patch it for me Missy," he directed to Melissa.

"I c-can't. I'll get sick."

Polanski strained to look over his right shoulder. The 7.62mm slug had passed through the cheek of his right buttocks. Blood streamed from entrance and exit wounds. He opened two field dressing packets while Bashir hurtled the jeep down the road.

"Just squeeze a tube full of this antibiotic cream into each hole and cover them with these gauze pads."

Melissa's face lost all of its color and she swallowed heavily. She complied with the instructions, no matter how reluctantly. When she finished, Melissa leaned far over the side of the jeep and vomited. Polanski pulled up his pants. When the girl recovered he patted her cheek.

"Good girl. Here, take a pull on this." He handed her a goatskin of *tibra*.

Melissa put the spout to her lips, swallowed, made a face. "Ugh! That's ghastly."

"Beer's beer, sweetheart. If you don't want any more, hand it to me."

"Was all that killing necessary back there?" Melissa addressed her question to the white-haired man in front of her.

"Would you rather they blew us away?" Before she could reply, Stonewall went on. "A bullet doesn't know you're on the other side, Melissa."

"But I'm not," she protested. "At least I'm neutral."

"Are you really?"

"Yes. Since back at that . . . place. It's all so *sordid*. I don't know what to believe any more." Again she buried her face in her hands and sobbed.

"We should be near the border, *effendi*.." Bashir looked forward again in time to navigate a slight curve in the road.

"Yeah. And there are our friends." Two hundred meters away, the other jeep sat at the side of the road. The squarish body tilted skyward at the left rear. Someone crouched by the tire, changing a flat. A short distance away, near the above-ground oil pipeline, two men struggled. Stonewall recognized the tall, lean frame of Marc Tolliver.

Tolliver shoved his opponent away from him. He drew a .45 automatic from a shoulder holster and pumped two rounds into the man's chest. The sound of the reports was distorted by doppler effect as Stonewall's jeep raced toward the turncoat. Stonewall turned to his left and yelled above the engine roar.

"When Bashir stops, everyone out and take cover behind the jeep."

Howard Byrd abandoned his repair job the moment he heard the approaching engine. He stood and reached into the rear of the jeep. He brought out a Uzi and fumbled with the cocking knob.

"Wouldn't you fucking know it," Stonewall griped aloud to himself when he recognized the weapon. Bashir stepped on the brake pedal and cramped the wheel.

The jeep slid broadside to the road and came to a halt. Five people leaped to the road. Bashir failed to move fast enough. A line of 9mm bullets from the Uzi, that punched through the windshield, stitched a path across his back. He sprawled on the blacktop in a spreading pool of blood.

"Not fair," Bashir protested in weak, blood-bubbled English. "They . . . didn't let me . . . do the . . . death scene from . . . *The Cowboys.*" Bashir Fawzi shuddered and lay still.

Wild fire from Stonewall and Polanski cracked around Byrd. He ducked and scrambled for protection under the jacked-up jeep. More slugs sprayed sand in his eyes before he rolled to safety on the opposite side. Burning grains stung his eyes. He dropped the Uzi and rubbed his fists into the agonized flesh. Marc Tolliver, who had run back to the disabled vehicle when he saw Stonewall's approach, grabbed up the small submachine gun and directed a burst at his pursuers.

Metal clanged and sang from impacts and ricochets. Stonewall changed hands with the Sidewinder and rotated the magazine to point to one right. Lefthanded he poked the short snout around the front tire and sent a three round burst at the blurred image of Marc Tolliver.

He missed.

At ninety meters the sub-guns didn't do well unless carefully aimed. Stonewall had no time for that. Polanski plunked a solid hit into the hood, near Tolliver's head. The slender turncoat abandoned his cover in panic. He ran back toward the pipeline. Stonewall leaped up and charged after him.

"Give me some covering fire," he shouted over one shoulder.

Polanski and Tex Nichols obliged, while Stonewall rapidly closed the distance between him and Tolliver. The former Special Forces major paused long enough to rip off a long burst at Stonewall, which smashed into his own jeep. Stonewall cracked out a single shot, followed by a three round burst. Tolliver ran on, circling wide to avoid a sump basin, used to handle overflow when the oil line was repressurized. Stonewall pounded after him.

"Tolliver, I've got a message for you from Trojan."

"Fuck Jackson Kurin and all the rest of you super-patriots."

"Funny, that's what he told me you were to do to yourself." Stonewall raised the Sidewinder and took deliberate aim at Tolliver's chest.

Marc Tolliver squeezed the trigger on the Uzi. The little Israeli SMG barked twice, sending plumes of sand into the air near Stonewall's feet, then went dry. Stonewall's finger twitched.

A neat triangle of 9mm holes appeared above the place where Tolliver's burst heart had previously functioned normally. The turncoat's legs went rubbery. He dropped the Uzi and fell into the sand.

"Stonewall, look out!" Hank Polanski yelled from behind him.

Barry the Bird had clawed the sand from his eyes and now rushed at Stonewall, a Browning Hi Power in one hand spitting slugs.

The high penetration 9mm bullets pierced the pipeline, releasing three thin, arching streams of crude oil. Another struck sparks from a ricochet of a huge valve wheel. Fumes began to accumulate in the still afternoon air. Stonewall whirled and dropped to one knee. He started to return fire.

Byrd blazed away, his blurry vision robbing him of accuracy. More sparks flew. Suddenly a brilliant ball of flame engulfed the pipeline. The powerful whoosh of the explosion knocked Stonewall face-first into the sand. Howard Byrd stumbled to a halt. He raised the Hi Power for a final triumphant shot into the back of Stonewall's head before he discovered he had emptied the magazine. With a yell of frustration, he leaped on the prostrate man.

A gust of breath grunted out of Stonewall when Howard Byrd's knees landed in the middle of his back, two inches above his kidneys. He also felt the stinging impact when Byrd's Browning struck his head, gouging skin and hair from the left side and his ear. A festive pyrotechnic display exploded inside his skull along with intense pain. It took Stonewall's total concentration to muster his forces and roll over. Byrd sprawled across his body.

Immediately Stonewall sat up. The receiver of the Sidewinder was clogged with sand. Byrd recovered himself and pulled an idiot TV stunt. He threw his Browning at Stonewall, who easily ducked it.

Byrd gathered his feet under him and sprang at Stonewall. The force of his charge carried them both over the lip of the seepage pool. The slippery black, viscous liquid closed over them. Byrd's hands churned as he tried to strangle Stonewall while attempting to force his head under the oil. The rugged, wiry soldier of fortune brought up a knee and connected solidly with Byrd's crotch.

Barry the Bird sucked air through the tiny "O" the pain had puckered his mouth into. His grasp faltered and he fell to the side. "Why, Stonewall?" Byrd gasped through the torment radiating from his groin. "You got the bomb factory, you bastard. Why come after me?"

"Trojan's contract called for wiping out the factory and terminate the three of you. I got Guterrez and Tolliver. Now it's your turn."

"Jesus Christ!" Byrd wailed. He groped at his waist and produced a custom-made Al Mar fighting knife. He got to his knees and lunged at Stonewall

The assegai hissed like an asp when Stonewall drew it from the bull-hide scabbard. Byrd's eyes widened at sight of it, though it didn't slow his attack. He flicked his 154cm blade forward and forced Stonewall to retreat. The soldier of fortune slipped in the oil and went to all fours.

Instantly Byrd came to his feet, his knife clutched in strong fingers, raised high over his head, poised to plunge into Stonewall's unprotected back. Byrd took a shuffling step forward. The blade started to descend.

Then Stonewall struck!

Assegai steel plunged deeply into Howard Byrd's abdomen. The shock of the massive wound paralyzed him. His mouth worked but no sound came. The Al Mar fighter dropped from numbed fingers. Stonewall gave a ruthless twist to the Zulu stabbing spear and reached out with his other hand to throw Byrd off his feet.

When Barry the Bird struck the surface, a huge wave rocked over the thick oil. Stonewall's powerful fingers clamped on the turncoat's jaw and slowly forced Byrd's head under the surface.

At last Howard Byrd's body responded to the massive injury done it. He tried to suck in badly needed air with which to rally his waining powers, only to fill his lungs with rich, black Libyan crude.

When Byrd's body stopped convulsing, Stonewall climbed to his feet, recovered his assegai and sloshed to the edge of the pool. Oil dripped from him and his eyes seemed abnormally white in his smeared face. Polanski, who had been studying the horizon through a pair of binoculars, turned to him and raised a clenched fist, which he pumped rapidly up and down in the old infantryman's signal to hurry up.

"Company comin', Cap'n. Looks like the whole fuckin' Libyan border detachment."

Stonewall began a stumbling run toward the jeep.

Chapter Nineteen

"We're still some fifteen miles from Capuzzo," Stonewall observed, thinking through his plans aloud. "We can buy a little time by taking the work road along the pipeline." He accepted the binoculars from Polanski and studied the force racing toward them from the border town. Satisfied, he handed them back.

"Most of those rigs can't do well off the road. They'll have to complete both sides of the triangle to come after us. If we can pile up a couple of miles lead we can angle across the desert to Egypt. All we'll have to contend with then are the four wheel drive jobs and that armored personnel carrier. Tex, you take the wheel." Stonewall shrugged out of his oil-sodden clothes and reached into his backpack for replacements. He regretted the damage to his soft, pliable pair of jump boots, companions that had been with him a long time. Perhaps they would come out of it. While he dressed, Polanski made a l conic observation.

"I just thought of something. Back there is Tobruk, where Rommel's *Afrika Korps* got its ass kicked. You don't think we're in for the same, do you, Cap'n?"

"You're a regular ray of sunshine, Polanski," Stonewall snapped. He turned to the silent, huddled form of Melissa Gould. "Are you all right, Melissa?"

"I . . . yes . . . I don't know. I have a lot of thinking to do."

"Hang in there. We'll be out of this in another half hour. Get his thing moving, Tex."

Despite the pain of his wound, Polanski manned his post behind the big Russian machinegun. It hurt too damned much to sit down, he declared. Unbidden, Melissa Gould dragged the last box of ammunition for the KPV into position so that Polanski would not have to strain himself bending over. He gave her a grateful smile.

A rapid dash down the maintenance road gained them a fraction over three miles lead, Stonewall estimated when he signaled Tex Nichols to pull off the road and start across the rugged terrain toward the Egyptian border. Heading east again, he watched two dark spots pull out of the column of pursuing Libyans and streak toward them. A grim smile replaced the frown on the soldier for hire's face.

Trust Qaddafi's desert lice to screw it up. Only two acceptable off-road vehicles. Then the APC joined the chase.

When the pursuers closed to maximum range for the KPV, Stonewall had Tex Nichols turn to face the oncoming enemy and stop. Polanski opened up with the Soviet KPV. At a mile and a half, the heavy slugs splashed sand high into the air and a few lucky hits ruined the radiator of one Land Rover. The occupants jumped aboard the armored personnel carrier and continued the chase. Tex started up again and the jeep put a rooster-tail of gritty particles into a boil behind them. Five miles closer to Egypt narrowed their lead to less than a mile.

"All right, let's give them another dose," Stonewall commanded.

Polanski hosed down the APC this time, the shorter range allowing greater accuracy. Three figures toppled from the slab sides of the armored vehicle and lay still on the ground. The main disadvantage to this improved gunnery quickly manifested itself.

A cottony puff of smoke appeared at the muzzle of the 57mm gun in the front of the APC a second before the crack of the blast reached their ears. The round fell short.

"Move out," Stonewall told Nichols.

"Choppers." Polanski pointed to the sky.

Don't let it be gunships, Stonewall thought prayerfully. The fat, locust-bodied craft hovered and paralleled their course, but did not close in. That didn't rule out troops, Stonewall reminded himself.

"Aren't we in Egypt by now?" Melissa inquired after

216

casting a fearful glance at the continued pursuit.

"We should be," Tex Nichols responded.

"But . . . they're still coming after us." A note of wonder sounded in her voice.

Nichols bounded the jeep over a sharp escarpment and sailed through the air for thirty feet before landing with a kidney-punishing crash. The right rear wheel struck a large, exposed rock, followed by a metallic crack and grating noise.

"There went the axle," Nichols announced. "This is as far as we go, kiddies."

Stonewall made a quick assessment of their ammunition situation. "Okay. We'll set up defensive positions along that ridge. Split up the grenades, there's six apiece. Hank, stay with that KPV. Maybe you can keep the choppers from landing or knock out any reinforcements."

"Do you expect me to fight?" Melissa quiried.

"You will if you want to stay alive," Stonewall snapped.

A frown cleft a furrow between Melissa's dark brows. "I think I can shoot Hank's rifle."

"Good girl! Let's shag it."

Stonewall scooped out a shallow parapit in the sand. He laid the six grenades in a line in front of him and looked to see Melissa doing her best to mimic his efforts. He allowed himself a small smile of satisfaction. All the while the choppers hovered out of range and waited for the arrival of ground forces.

When the APC and remaining jeep arrived, the helicopters descended. They disgorged a platoon of troops.

"*Gary Owen, Gary Owen, Gary Owen,*" Polanski sang in an off-key baritone. "*In that valley of Montana all alone. There are better days to be for the Seventh Cavalry . . .*" He gave the defenders a lopsided grin.

Melissa gave Stonewall a pained look. "He can't help his sick sense of humor." Stonewall raised his voice. "After all, he *was* a sergeant major."

A nervous titter escaped from Melissa's lips before she realized that Stonewall had managed, at least in part, to coax her out of her fear. Her eyes widened, though, then the Libyans began to advance.

Flashes came from the ACP's main gun and machineguns snarled in support of the approach over open ground. The 57mm shells began to explode in the depression behind the ridge. Tensely the defenders waited.

Finally the strain became too much for Melissa. She opened fire, on semi-auto, with Polanski's M-14. The first wild, unaimed shots didn't even cause the Libyan soldiers to duck. Then a man went down, clutching at his left calf. Unaccountably, Stonewall felt a touch of pride.

"Good shooting!" he called over the increasing sounds of battle.

"Damn," Melissa retorted. "I was aiming for his chest."

"Did your father teach you how to shoot?"

"No. I learned in the SDS."

The admission crumpled all the warmth of Stonewall's good feelings. *Peace* advocates they called themselves. The advancing troops had closed to under a hundred meters. Stonewall took aim with Bashir's AK-47 and ripped off a five round burst.

Three men folded at the middle and pitched into the sand.

Stonewall threw a grenade. In mid-hurl his eye caught movement in the sky. "Another chopper," he yelled down to Polanski. "This one's coming our way."

The grenade detonated, drowning out Polanski's reply. He swung the KPV, though, and lined up on the new target. It had to be a gunship, Polanski realized as he pressed the firing stud. A line of steel-jacketed death reached out for the rapidly swelling ship. Polanski consumed a good half of his remaining ammunition, cross-hatching the deadly gunship, before it lurched and gyrated to the ground. The crash sent up a huge billow of black smoke, interlaced with licking tongues of blue-white flame. Two more choppers appeared behind where it had fallen from.

"Oh, shit, we've had it now," Polanski spoke to himself. He continued to fire until he exhausted his last round. One helicopter wavered, righted itself and came on. The other began to swing into line to deliver a devastating blast from its mini-gun. On the ground the Libyan troops got within twenty-five yards of the scant defense put up by Stonewall and his companions.

Another grenade, then another. Stonewall continued to pitch the smooth spheres until he held the last one. Above the gunship adjusted position to fire. Suddenly the ground trembled with growing violence and an interceptor flashed past, its afterburner uttering a banshee wail. Twin smoking trails streaked from under its wings and the helicopter gunship disappeared in an expanding ball of smoke and fire. On the tail of the attacking jet, Stonewall recognized the star and crescent emblem of Egypt. The soldier of fortune reared up and emptied the last magazine for the AK into five Libyans, braver than the rest, who had reached the crest.

Stonewall dropped the Kalashnikov and swung his Sidewinder into line while with the other hand he drew his assegai. If he was going down, by God, he'd smoke every one of these bastards he could on the way.

A loud *thwop-thwop* of helicopter blades sounded from behind. The Libyans had managed to encircle them! Stonewall hazarded a quick glance in that direction and saw two, then three, no five choppers settling to the ground. From the open waist doors leaped a reinforced company of Egyptian troops. Stonewall threw back his head and bellowed his eerie Rebel yell. The Sidewinder blazed.

Two more Libyans crumpled into bleeding heaps.

Stonewall swung his assegai and another desert louse stopped fighting and tried to stuff coils of intestine back into his slashed abdomen. Stonewall backhanded it and smacked a deep crevass in the skull of a fourth Libyan. Then the troopers of the Egyptian special air assault group swarmed past the struggling soldier of fortune, driving the Libyans before them.

The jet returned and reduced the APC to smoldering ruin. Then Eric Bach appeared beside Stonewall, casually snapping off shots from a .458 Winchester African at targets of opportunity. How the hell could the little guy withstand all that recoil? Stonewall wondered.

"Fine sport, what?" Eric asked in an affected British accent.

"W-where did you come from? How about all," Stonewall waved his arm to indicate the Egyptian regulars.

"The Egyptian government takes an extremely dim view of such war-like violations of its borders. All I had to do was suggest to them that some such enterprise was afoot and they took care of the rest."

Stonewall turned away from the dwindling battle and walked down-slope to the ruined jeep, Eric at his side. Melissa trailed them, looking green about the lips in contrast to her ashen cheeks. Ted Swink and the lovely Patty Sayers waited there, talking with Polanski.

"Glad you could drop by," Stonewall began dryly.

"Any time," Patty remarked.

"Hey, do you know what that Libyan troop leader said when he saw us coming?" Ted Swink asked, then went on before anyone could reply. " 'Look at all them fuckin' Indians.' "

"Please, I've had all the Custer jokes I can take in one day," Stonewall retorted.

Swink sobered, all business. "I have a private communication for you from Trojan." He handed Stonewall a sealed envelope.

Stonewall extracted a pocket knife and slit the seals.

He unfolded a single page of thick, creamy buff paper and read the few lines written there. A scowl hardened into smoldering anger. Without comment, Stonewall refolded the page and inserted it in the envelope. Then he made introductions around, omitting the name of Melissa's employer.

Eric Bach produced a bottle of Johnnie Walker Black and handed it to Stonewall. "Time we head for Cairo."

"I'll second that," Stonewall injected between swallows.

"I won't be seeing you again?" Melissa Gould asked Stonewall in his hotel room in Cairo early the next afternoon.

It seemed he was always saying good-bye to good-looking women. "I suppose not. Are you going to write the story?"

"You bet your ass I am. I . . ." she hesitated. "I can't tell you how much of a fool I feel, Stonewall. When a person sees everything they've ever believed in turned to shit."

Stonewall reached out and drew her unresisting body to his. "Hey, cut the Lib Lady talk and kiss me."

Melissa did.

Stonewall's big hands slid up under her wooly dacron sweater and closed over the soft, yielding mounds of her breasts. Maybe there was something to the Burn the Bra Movement, he thought. His thumbs began to tease her generous nipples, which hardened in eager response. Melissa moaned against his mouth and her tongue darted past his teeth. Their passionate osculation ended in mutual gasps.

Melissa began to undress the rugged man who held her so tightly. "Oh, hurry. Your plane leaves in . . ."

"Ten hours," he completed for her.

"That's nowhere near enough time," she protested. "Oh, I'm gonna get that hypocrite bastard Qaddafi. I'm gonna get him good."

"Your boss might not like an article slanted that way."

"So what? I'll get it published somewhere."

"In *Spotlight?*" Stonewall suggested half teasingly.

"*Spotlight?* Ugh!" Melissa's face made a sudden, dramatic change. "Awh, darling, there's so many things I'm going to have to relearn. No more business talk. The lady wants to be loved."

Stonewall gave her his most winning smile. "The gentleman is most happy to oblige." He slid out of his undershorts.

"Oh, my, that's a most dramatic weapon you carry," Melissa cooed.

Stonewall lifted her in his arms and carried her to the bed. "All the better to wound you with, my dear."

"Welcome to Southern California," the head stewardess announced over the intercom of the 747. "The temperature in Los Angeles is eighty-four degrees, with no wind, under partially cloudy skies. There is a first level smog alert and no rain is forecast. On behalf of Captain Smith and . . ." Stonewall tuned her out.

He glanced across the aisle to where Polanski and Ted Swink sat in close conversation. Suddenly his discomfort, which had steadily increased during the long, round-about flight back to the States, intensified. They would be on the ground in a couple of minutes.

"International passengers will deplane through the customs area," the cabin attendant continued.

Whee! He could hardly wait. He should feel something. Anticipation? Pride? Stonewall chided himself for his empty attitude. It had to be the information he carried with him from Trojan. The revelation had ruined his day. And many a more, he reflected bitterly.

When the jumbo jet taxied to the ramp and shut down, Stonewall waited with the other first class passengers until the eager coach sitters left the aircraft. He, Polanski and Swink ambled to the customs shed and identified their luggage on one of a dozen long, stainless steel covered tables. They waited their turn, assured the blue-uniformed agent they had nothing to declare and stepped into the smoggy atmosphere of a nation, supposedly at peace. To Stonewall it felt like hell.

"There's supposed to be a rental car for us on the third level over there," Ted Swink informed them. He started away from the terminal, toward the narrow island with its peak-roofed shelters for waiting bus passengers and beyond to the towering gray concrete edifice of a parking garage. Stonewall caught Polanski by the arm and held him back. From his pocket he produced the letter from Trojan. Polanski took it and read. Hidden in a seemingly innocuous communication was another, sinister message.

" 'The bearer,' " Polanski quietly read aloud. He glanced up at Swink. " 'The bearer is our leak. Sorry about this, Stonewall, but I want you to terminate him with extreme prejudice. Trojan.' How are we gonna do it?"

"I have it figured out. Follow my lead."

Up on the third level, at the rental car, Stonewall produced his silver hip flask. He unscrewed the cap and offered it to Ted Swink. "Here. Let's have one for a job well done."

"Christ," Swink protested. "I thought we had enough of those on the plane." Swink, visibly nervous, had consumed far more than the two soldiers of fortune.

"Naw, c'mon, Ted," Stonewall began in a palsy tone. "Just one more. The fuzz out here in California are hell on drunk drivers, so we won't have another chance before Hank and I catch our flight to Charlotte."

"I really don't think I should. I have to drive to a meeting in Beverly Hills."

Polanski stepped behind Swink and clamped his arms to his sides in a massive bear hug. "You're not being sociable, fellah," he grunted through the effort of restraining the struggling man.

"Who are you going to see, Swink?" Stonewall inquired in a taunting tone. "Qaddafi's surrogate, Imhammad Jalluud?" Stonewall forced the neck of the flask between

223

Swink's lips. "Drink you turncoat mother-fucker. Drink until it runs out your fuckin' ears."

Swink fought them the best he could. His crying need for a breath of air defeated him. His throat constricted and he swallowed a fiery trail of scotch. Only when the pint flask gurgled dry did he manage to suck in a protracted draught of welcome Los Angeles smog. In mid-gulp, Polanski jerked him off his feet. Stonewall took his legs and the duo began to sidestep toward the concrete parapet.

"No!" Swink bleated when the realization of their intentions penetrated his alcohol-fogged brain. "Oh, noo-o-o-o-o!"

With a nod from Stonewall, he and Polanski heaved Ted Swink over the side.

He screamed all the way to the ground.

Stonewall opened the door of the light blue Ford rental. "Well, back to Fayetteville."

"Yeah. I got a lotta beer drinkin' to catch up on."

"And I've got a little souvenir of Libya for Karol," Stonewall told his companion. A bulging erection, he completed in his thoughts.